Serpent's Keep Two
The Six Temples

David R. Beshears

Greybeard Publishing
Washington State

Greybeard Publishing
P.O. Box 480
McCleary, WA 98557-0480

ISBN 978-1-947231-01-6

Serpent's Keep Two

The Six Temples

Chapter One

The small room held a narrow cot and a tiny side table. There was an unlit oil lamp on the table, the only light in the room coming from a small, square window that was set high on the wall. In the wall opposite the window was a heavy wooden door bound with iron straps and hung on iron hinges.

Jacob Quigley was asleep on the cot under a drab-green blanket. He woke slowly and rolled onto his back. He opened his eyes and stared blankly up at the ceiling. He blinked, rubbed his face and looked sharply again at the ceiling.

He recognized that ceiling.

He pulled the blanket off and sat up, looked curiously about the room. He was in a monk cell in the temple.

The temple. Jake was home.

That's impossible. How can I be home?

He stood up, shrugged a sore shoulder and looked again about the small cell. His jacket was hanging on a hook beside the door. He looked down at his clothes then. He was wearing the same clothes that he had been wearing the last he could recall.

He found his boots under the cot, put them on and tied up the laces. He went to the door then and pushed down on the heavy, iron latch. The door opened easily and he stepped out into the hall.

Jake was definitely in the temple. He was home. Serpent's Keep was less than a day's hike away.

He had no idea how he got there. The last thing he remembered, he and his uncle Tobias had come out of a gateway side-passage and had just started across an empty world of drifting gray fog.

What happened?

He followed the narrow hall to the wider corridor that ran the length of this wing of the temple. Reaching the front foyer, he met Brother John and another monk just coming in through the front door, both dressed in plain, heavy monks' robes.

Brother John gave his companion a nod of dismissal and turned to Jake.

"Brother Jacob," he said with a patient smile. "It is good to see you up. How do you feel?"

"Confused," said Jake.

John indicated the passage directly ahead and they started into it.

"I'm sure it will all sort itself out," he said as they walked.

"Uh, huh," said Jake. "How did I get here?"

"I couldn't say," said John. "Are you hungry?"

Jake realized then that he was. "A bit, yes."

"This way, then." John guided Jake into the dining hall and to a nearby table. The hall was nearly empty, with lunch just finishing. John caught the attention of a monk standing at the small buffet who was beginning to clear things away. The man nodded and began preparing a plate for Jake.

"I'll let Master Peter know that you're up and about," said John.

"All right," said Jake. "And he'll know how I got here?"

"He has been eager to speak with you."

Jake noted silently that John had avoided answering his question. He watched him leave the hall and then gave a polite smile to the monk bringing his plate and a glass of water.

"Thank you," he said.

The monk nodded in reply and returned to clearing away the buffet. Jake ate in silence. After several minutes he found himself alone in the hall. He had finished his meal and was taking his plate to the return window when Master Peter came into the room.

"Ah, Brother Jacob. Welcome home." Peter was in his sixties, but despite his graying hair could have passed for a man much younger.

"Thank you, Master Peter." They shook hands, and then Jake stepped over to the buffet table. He refilled his glass from a water pitcher. "I must tell you, I'm surprised to find myself here."

"Is that so?"

"Yes." Jake stared at his water glass, set it down on the table beside the pitcher. "I don't suppose you can shed any light on how I got here?"

"Very little, I'm afraid." Master Peter indicated the nearest table and they sat down facing one another. "I was in fact hoping that you might regale and enlighten me with tales of your adventures these past seven months."

Seven months...

"Seven? Really?" Jake hadn't realized that so much time had passed in the worlds outside the passageways. It certainly didn't jive with his internal calendar.

"Seven months and a handful of days," said Peter. "Miss Meara Gyles told us of your sacrifice in closing the gates, though she had no doubt that we would one day see you again."

"I had enough doubt of my own for everyone," said Jake. "And I have no idea how I ended up here."

"We found you unconscious on the front steps," said Master Peter. "Near sunset last evening."

"And Uncle Tobias?"

"Tobias?" asked Peter. "You've been with Brother Tobias?"

"We've been traveling the side-passages," said Jake. "Last I remember, we came out of a passage... we were in a landing..." Jake frowned, struggled to remember. He looked up at Peter. "Tobias and I were together."

"I'm sorry, Jacob. You were alone when we found you." Peter managed a smile then. "I am pleased to hear that Tobias is alive."

"Presenter of good tidings," said Jake tiredly. "That's me."

"These *side-passages*... they are related to the gateways, I assume?"

"Kind of," said Jake, shrugging. "They are very limited in where they go, and until recently each was confined to a single world."

"I see." Peter looked thoughtfully at Jake. "And they didn't shut down when you closed the gates?"

"Only the main passages closed. Good thing. I found Tobias at a landing between side-passages."

"Fortuitous, indeed."

"Janice," Jake said suddenly.

"Excuse me?"

"Tobias' nemesis, you might say; more so even than Marcus. She is more of a threat, for sure."

"And she—"

"We think she's creating them," said Jake. "Passages."

"Such a thing is possible?"

"Honestly, I don't know. Even Tobias can't say for sure, but something is happening. Janice knows the science of the gateways better than anyone alive, enough to make her dangerous."

"And she is out there now?"

Janice had been trapped in the side-passages when Jake shut down the gates. The Other Worlds were now isolated from one another, and even the side-passages were supposed to be limited to their individual worlds.

"She's looking for a way out," he said. *And a way to reopen the gateways.*

"You found a way out," said Peter. "Clearly. You are here."

"Clearly? Apparently, at most." Jake grew retrospective. When he spoke again, his words were distant. "Tobias and I had come onto a landing. It was empty... I heard something; like wind. A strange wind. And then... then I was here."

Master Peter reached out and placed a hand on Jake's arm.

"As you have returned to us, I am confident that we will soon be enjoying the company of Brother Tobias." Peter stood then, rested his hand heavily on Jake's shoulder. "You are welcome to stay as long you feel need. We will talk again."

"Thanks," said Jake. "I'll be heading to Serpent's Keep in the morning."

"Of course." Peter gave Jake a final pat on the shoulder and started away. "I'll see you at dinner. I would hear more of your adventure."

Jake stepped out of the trailhead and approached the wooden west gate, set into the rough stone wall that enclosed the village of Serpent's Keep. He pulled on a metal ring, listened to the peal of the bell on the other side of the wall. Several moments later he heard the voice of the guard on watch.

"Can I help you?"

"Sure can," said Jake. "Jacob Quigley. I'd like to get inside, please."

"Jacob Quig—" There was a long hesitation. "Are you sure?"

"Um... pretty sure..."

Another long hesitation, and then Jake heard the wooden beam slide aside and the gate opened.

"Sorry," said the young man on watch. As a member of the Citizen's Watch, he was unarmed and dressed in civilian clothes. "You took me by surprise, Mister Quigley."

"Oh, I hear ya'," said Jake. He mumbled over his shoulder as he started down the alleyway, swathed in shadow. "I'm still gettin' over the surprise myself."

Reaching the main thoroughfare, he stopped at the corner and took in the sight. It was early evening, and it was quiet at this end of the small village. The main gate was a short distance to his right, the heart of the village to his left. There was a small group of people gathered outside the café several hundred yards into the village.

He crossed the avenue and started up the street, walking into the village proper, He passed the park plaza and turned into the narrow side road where the Quigley Estate waited.

The gate wasn't locked. He took the walk and the steps up to the front door. The door was locked, and he lifted and dropped the door knocker. He stared at the dragon knocker and waited. It was almost a minute before the door opened and Mr. Griffin stood looking down at him. Only the briefest of emotion washed across Mr. Griffin's face, then the man's mouth and eyes locked into their more familiar state of formal dispassion.

Or at least he tried.

"Master Jacob," Mr. Griffin said calmly. "I am... pleased... to see you."

"You and me both," said Jake. He pointed inside, past Mr. Griffin. "Um..."

"But of course," Griffin said quickly, stepping back and to one side. "My apologies."

Once inside, with the front door closed to the world outside, Jake looked about the room, quietly absorbing the comforting atmosphere of the Quigley Estate.

He turned about and gave a contented sigh.

"No place like home, Mr. Griffin," he said. "I never thought I'd see the old place again."

"There was never a doubt, sir."

Jake looked side-glance at Mr. Griffin. "Really?" he asked doubtfully.

Griffin now managed a trace of humor. "Miss Gyles wouldn't allow it."

"That sounds like Meara," said Jake. "So I'm not dead then?" His uncle Tobias' death had been declared in much less time than this.

"Presumed only," said Mr. Griffin. "There was nothing official."

"Good. I bet the paperwork to bring me back would have been a nightmare. Which reminds me... have you seen Uncle Tobias?"

The question managed to startle Mr. Griffin. "Should we have? Is he—"

"He is." Jake indicated that they should head into the kitchen. Once there, he set about getting a glass of water, sat then at the island counter as he ate fruit from the bowl.

Fresh fruit; in their travels these past months, food choices had often been limited. They ate what they found, any extra they carried with them for the scarce times to come.

There had been more than a few of those.

No need to bring that up just now. He took another bite of the apple, told Mr. Griffin how he had found Tobias after closing Serpent's Gate, how together they had found and then began traveling side-passages. They spent months following the trail of Janice while always on the lookout for a way out of the passages.

"And so you have. What of Master Quigley?"

"The last thing I remember before waking up at the Temple was stepping out of a side-passage into a gray, empty place, and Tobias was right beside me. I think I heard something, like wind... but I can't be sure. Next thing I know, I'm waking up in a monk cell. Peter says they found me on the front steps."

"And no sign of Master Quigley..."

"Nope."

Mrs. Hodges came in through the back door. Seeing Jake, the expression on her face changed from anxious to delight.

"So it's true then!" she exclaimed.

"Hey, Mrs. H." They met in the middle of the kitchen and hugged. Mrs. Hodges stepped back to get a better look at Jake.

"Word is all through the village... young Quigley has come home." she said, still smiling broadly. "Wasn't sure to believe it, but here you are."

"Yes, Ma'am."

The tall double-doors opened ahead of Tobias Quigley and he stepped through and into the large audience chamber. The strong scent of dragon filled the great hall, the walls to either side lined with every species of Jahai, the varied inhabitants of the four habitable planets of the Jahai system.

Tobias continued down the center of the chamber, walking steadily past the dragons and on toward the raised wooden platform at the far end of the room. Tobias was in his late fifties, with rugged features and bushy salt and pepper hair.

He reached the platform and looked up at Natan, the Jahai ruler. Natan was of the Bentai Jahai. The Bentai were much more humanoid in physical appearance than other Jahai species. Natan was just a head taller than the average human, with sloping shoulders, a large head and protruding snout. He had extraordinarily long fingers ending in curved black claws. As most Bentai, he was dressed in an open leather vest and a calf-length skirt.

"So good to see you, our friend Tobias Quigley," said Natan. His voice was smooth, his words clear and precise.

Tobias gave a slight nod, briefly held out his palms. "Dear friend Natan, sovereign guide of the Jahai."

Natan held out a clawed hand, turned it palm up and then drew it back. He rested the hand on the arm of the heavy wooden throne. At that gesture, Tobias took a step forward, stood now directly at the base of the platform.

"I thank you for your welcoming salutation," he said.

"It has been many cycles since you last walked this hall, friend Tobias."

"Due to circumstances rather beyond my control, friend Natan," said Tobias.

"So I understand. I was pleased when I heard that you were yet among us." Natan looked aside, lifted a hand and gave a signal to a Jahai standing just off the platform, another of the Bentai. He turned again to Tobias. "Come sit with me. We have much to discuss, I should think."

Tobias stepped up onto the platform as a chair suitable for humans was brought up and placed beside Natan's throne. Tobias sat in the chair, made himself comfortable and looked about the chamber. The Jahai in the hall had begun to settle back into their stations, seeing that Natan and Tobias would likely be in quiet conversation for some time.

As was often the case when friend Tobias Quigley visited.

"My feelings go one way and then another, Tobias," said Natan. "To close Serpent's Gate, to seal it for all time; to isolate our worlds, all worlds."

"We suspected the day would come, Natan."

"Perhaps we did. Yes, perhaps we did."

"I do understand."

The conversation drifted then to the Rhetani, the threat that had caused the closing of the gates. The Rhetani had always been there, had been the reason for originally dividing and dispersing the artifacts.

And then the threat had become more imminent. The Rhetani would bring all the worlds under their control.

The conversation then fell to matters more immediate.

"Janice is out there still," said Natan. It was an observation more than a question.

"That she is," said Tobias. "We have been following her trail."

"You and your blood," said Natan. "Jake."

"My nephew, yes."

"You will find her; you and your... *nephew.*"

"We must."

"What will you do with her, friend Tobias?" Natan asked calmly. "How can we help you?"

Tobias had trapped Janice in a side-passage landing long ago, back when he separated the gate into individual artifacts that he then scattered across the Other Worlds.

He had hoped that she would exist there for all time. But she had somehow managed to gain her freedom, had brought together others of the Rhetani in her search of the artifacts, threatening all worlds. To defend against this threat, Serpent's Gate had been sealed, forever isolating the Other Worlds from one another.

It was now feared that even that had not been enough. Janice had abilities beyond any human, beyond any Jahai.

"Janice needs to be rendered harmless," said Tobias.

Natan nodded slowly. "A secure confinement."

"Yes," said Tobias.

"I understand," said Natan.

Tobias stepped away from the Grand Hall, the massive doors closing behind him. The central plaza of the sprawling Village of the Dragons was open and spacious, surrounded by large structures that were set in amongst towering trees; beyond these to either side, great cliffs rose high into the sky.

The village was a sprawling community of large, stark, cavernous structures surrounded by a forest of massive trees and an open forest floor. It was one of only a few sites with hub landings, central locations reached by several side-passages.

Yet Tobias should not have been able to get to it from any passage that he and Jake had traveled since the closing of Serpent's Gate. The fact that he was there was at odds with everything that he knew of the side-passages.

Taking this, with his recent experiences, with the disappearance of young Jake, and with the disquieting news that Natan had just given him at the close of their conversation, all made Tobias more than a bit anxious.

Chapter Two

After a good night's sleep in his own bed and a
delicious breakfast prepared by Mrs. Hodges, Jake
spent a few hours in Tobias' library and in the hidden
command center. He had no idea what he was looking
for, rather hoped that it would jump out at him and cry
out *here's what happened to you, Jake!* to be quickly
followed by *here is how you find your uncle... yet again.*

Actually, he just wanted a clue. Such had happened
before. He needed to know what the first step was. After
that, the second step would show itself.

He found nothing.

Late morning, Jake left the estate; he wandered first
across the road to the town park. About a dozen people
were gathered around a group of picnic benches. It
looked like a family gathering. After watching from a
distance for a few minutes, he left the plaza and started
up the main thoroughfare.

There were quite a few villagers out and about. Most
gave Jake a smile and a nod, several wanted to stop
and say hello and welcome him home. He didn't know
most of them, but they recognized him.

He found Meara's mother at her booth in the
marketplace, where she sold kitchenware and assorted
utensils. He didn't know her very well, had really only

spoken to her a couple of times, but she apparently knew every detail of his journeys into the Outland and the Other Worlds. She had been kept fully up-to-date by Meara.

Mrs. Gyles also had been certain that they would see Jake again, having been so advised by her daughter.

As for Meara, she was going to be upset that she had missed his return. It was only then that Jake found that Meara was at the Farm, where she worked several days a week, necessary to supplement what she earned working part time at the Quigley Estate. She wouldn't be back in the village for several days.

Jake thanked Mrs. Gyles and wandered toward the exit of the marketplace. It was close enough to lunch that he decided to drop in to the cafe.

Entering the restaurant, he saw only one other patron. Jake gave a nod when the man looked up from his bowl of soup, then headed toward a table in the middle of the room.

"Jacob Quigley!" Sparta hurried from behind the counter. Jake braced himself as she reached him and gave him a powerful hug.

Well that was odd. They hadn't been on hugging terms before his disappearance.

"I heard you were back," she said.

"How are you, Sparta?" he asked awkwardly.

"Oh, you know," she said with a shrug. She indicated the nearest table, waited for him to sit down. "What can I get for you? It's on the house."

"That's very nice of you. Whatever's the special is fine," said Jake. "So long as there's no peas."

"You got it," Sparta said, grinning. She started away. "Coming right up."

Jake managed to relax then, called out to Sparta. "And how about some of that great coffee?"

"Absolutely, Jake."

Sparta gave Jake's order to Wallace and quickly returned with a cup and the carafe. As she poured his coffee, she began detailing the theories that folks had on what had happened to Jake and where he might have gone. From what he could tell, Meara had accurately described how he had disappeared when closing the gate, and had glowingly noted Jake's sacrifice. The theories as to what had happened next went all over the place, but they usually involved barren landscapes and feral creatures of the night.

Sparta was called away in mid-tale when a pair of customers entered the cafe. She returned a few minutes later with a bowl of soup and a small plate with two biscuits.

"The special of the day," she said. "And no peas."

He was halfway through his soup when Sheriff Smith came in. He worked his way to Jake's table, catching Sparta's attention before giving Jake a friendly smile.

"Mister Quigley. Mind if I sit down?"

"Not at all, Sheriff." Jake set his spoon down, picked up the last of a biscuit and tossed it into his mouth. "I recommend the soup."

"Perhaps I will." The sheriff slid the chair out and sat down. "I'll be having lunch a bit later."

Sparta returned with coffee. "How are you today, Sheriff?"

"I'm doing just fine, Sparta." He watched her fill his cup. "Thank you."

Sparta refilled Jake's coffee, gave him a wink and left the table. Jake lifted his cup to the sheriff.

"And the coffee is as good as I remember," he said.

"It is fine, at that." The sheriff took a cautious sip. "I understand you've had yourself quite the adventure. And you found your uncle, I hear."

"And you may also have heard that I've misplaced him."

"Not in quite those words. Still, great news that he's alive and kicking."

"The last I saw," said Jake. *He was right beside me...*

"You'll be going out again to find him, I imagine."

"Just as soon as I have an idea where to start looking."

"I'm sure that'll come." The sheriff gave a friendly grin. "You did it once before."

"I had clues before. Lots of 'em."

"Oh, I expect the clues will come soon enough." The sheriff gulped down his coffee and stood up. "Well, I just wanted to welcome you home and let you know that we're glad to see you back safe. And we're mighty grateful for the news about Tobias."

"Thank you, Sheriff," said Jake. "And my uncle's death certificate?"

Sheriff Smith gave Jake a sharp nod. "Not to worry. City Hall is already on it."

The sheriff passed Mr. Dante on his way out of the café, the bank owner arriving right on schedule for his daily lunch break. Seeing Jake, the banker stopped on his way to his traditional table along the back wall. After the briefest of welcomes, he advised Jake to drop by the bank at his convenience. While Mr. Griffin had never allowed young Master Quigley to be declared dead, there were nonetheless a few papers to review regarding the estate's ongoing financial arrangements.

Jake assured him that he would drop in later, at which Mr. Dante gave a deep bow of the head and continued on to his table.

Tobias approached the sturdy, circular building that was sitting to one side of the central plaza of the Jahai village. A pair of heavily muscled Thrauhm dragons stood watch, one to either side of the tall, wide opening that faced the plaza. The dragons shifted slightly at Tobias' approach, bowed briefly in acknowledgment and let him enter unchallenged.

The floor of the inner chamber was compact dirt. There were no windows and no other doors, and the chamber was empty but for a circle of six daises standing in the center of the room. A square stone, about twelve inches on a side, rested on each of the six platforms. Each stone was engraved with its own unique geometric symbol.

Tobias circled the daises, glancing at the symbols engraved on each *passage stone*. He found the one he wanted. He reached out and placed a hand on the stone.

He was immediately enveloped in blinding, empty white, awash in a rush of light and warped vision. He had been expecting it of course, but the onrush of the side-passage thread nonetheless made him dizzy and he stumbled forward when he came out on the other side.

He stood in a large clearing, a dais similar to the one he had just left standing nearby. The clearing was surrounded by a thick forest; towering cliffs rose hundreds of feet to either side. High above, seen between the tops of the cliffs, the midday sky was pale blue.

He was standing on the floor of the Great Ravine.

He shouldn't have been able to reach the Great Ravine directly from the Village of the Dragons. The village resided in a side-passage landing on another world entirely. Prior to shutting down the gates, the passage stone would have taken Tobias to another time and place in that Other World. In the past, it had always been three distinct steps to get from there to here, and that had been back when Serpent's Gate had been open.

Yet here he was. Natan had said this was so. The physical laws regarding side-passages made it impossible for it to be so. Something had changed. Something *was changing*. Someone was messing with the laws underlying the web of the universe.

The Jahai had identified a number of similar impossible and yet very real alterations to the universe over the past months. Tobias had direct experience with such occurrences, the most recent being when he and Jake had been separated, his nephew vanishing before his very eyes.

Janice was doing something very bad and it was shattering the universe.

§

The Farm was a sprawling two hundred acres of agricultural landscape surrounding a cluster of barns and assorted buildings. To anyone traveling the dirt road that ran alongside the western perimeter of the farm, the scene gave an impression of a still-life painting. Very little moved, very little changed.

In the heart of this still-life, Meara was helping tie down the tarp of the last in a line of four wagons that had been loaded with vegetables destined for Serpent's Keep. She and the others of the small work crew worked in silence, which only intensified the atmosphere of an *otherworld* that lay eerily over the farm.

Meara looked up from her work to the hollow, resonating sound of wooden wheels, iron axles and jostling sideboards. In the distance, a caravan of empty wagons was approaching, traveling up the road bordering the farm.

It was another work crew coming to harvest and pack vegetables and fruit to take back to the market.

The manager of the village Farm came out of one of the buildings and walked past the line of loaded wagons. He stood in front of the first and waited for the arriving caravan.

Charles Victor was a tall, slender man in his early sixties. He had been managing the farm for thirty years, and before that had been a fulltime farmhand. He had lived on the farm his entire life.

The lead wagon turned off the road and into the farm, and the caravan worked its way toward the compound. The man leading the caravan let the empty wagons continue on as he stepped aside to talk with the farm manager.

Charles smiled at some comment made by the wagonmaster. He looked briefly in Meara's direction before turning again to his conversation with the new arrival.

Their conversation finally finished, the wagonmaster followed after his caravan and Charles walked back to Meara.

"I expect you'll be eager to start back, Meara," he said. The comment was almost cheery, something Meara seldom saw from the farm manager.

"What's going on?" she asked.

"Your friend has returned."

"Sir?"

"Jacob Quigley."

"Master Jacob?"

"And if the rumors are to be believed, young Quigley found Tobias out there somewhere, though for some reason he didn't return with him." Charles looked up and down the line of fully loaded wagons. Catching the attention of the caravan's lead wagonmaster, he gave the go-ahead hand signal, looked again to Meara. "You have a safe trip back, Miss Gyles."

Dusk had come to the Great Ravine. Dark shadows crept out from the thick forest of evergreen and into the expansive clearing. Flying dragons appeared in the black hollows of cave openings set high in the cliff walls and leapt into the airspace above the forest canopy, drifted out above the treetops.

Tobias sat amongst a small gathering of dragons in the heart of the clearing. Many of the twelve species of Jahai were present, including several of the more humanoid Bentai dragons. One fed wood into a campfire in the center of the gathering. Tobias suspected the fire was for his benefit, as he knew campfires were rare in the ravine. While he had never put the Great Ravine on any map, he had visited there many times. It served primarily as an outpost for the sleek Lynhaur dragons, one of the flying Jahai, and was a landing with a minor side-passage gate to a landing in the distant past.

Looking about at the gathering now, he wondered aloud at the number of Jahai species that were present.

"We feel a disruption in the web," said one of the Bentai. "Many are anxious."

"Some have come to bear witness," said another.

"Some are not here by choice," said a third. "The threads were not intended to bring us here."

"Though all stand watch against what may come," said a dragon of the Thrauhm species, with strong reptilian features.

"I understand your unease," said Tobias. "I too have felt the disturbance."

"Why would the closing of the gate create such disruption in the passages, Tobias?" asked the Bentai dragon.

"It would not, my friend," said Tobias. "It did not."

"The Rhetani?" asked another.

"I fear so."

"Alone here... was sad," said a large, heavyset dragon. He had been trapped here when the Other World gates had closed, had not been able to return home. "Apart from brothers and sisters. Sad. This different. Worse than sad. Feel bad inside. This... bad."

New threads had been born from the disruptions of late, their origins unknown, and many were afraid to travel them. There had been stories.

And then most recently the story of Tobias and his travels with his nephew, their separation. Tobias mentioned as much.

"Was here," one dragon stated, unaccustomed to human speech.

"Excuse me?" Tobias wasn't sure what he had meant by that.

"Was here," he repeated. He lifted a clawed hand and pointed to the edge of the clearing. "Was there."

"You did not know?" asked one of the Bentai. "You were not told?"

"Apparently not, my friend," said Tobias. "To what are you referring?"

"Jacob Quigley, blood of Tobias, was found at the edge of the clearing. When we could not revive him, he was taken to the Temple to be cared for."

Chapter Three

Jake stepped out the door of the Adventurer's Guild and into the narrow side street. He started in the direction of the main thoroughfare. It was late afternoon, and the air was beginning to grow cool. He stuffed his hands into the pockets of his light jacket and pushed on.

The streets were lined with lamp posts, the lights mostly gas but there were also a few electric. The scattering of electric lights were already on. Jake passed a man standing beneath one of the gas lamps, lifting a rod to the globe. He gave Jake a mumbled '*good evening*' before lighting the lamp and moving on to the next.

Jake had spent the past hour at the Guild, talking with members about nothing in particular, hoping to catch some bit of news that might be a clue as to what he should do next. Perhaps someone had seen something in the Outland, heard of some strange sighting or event; perhaps the sudden appearance of a slightly graying, middle-aged gentleman...

As he had found during visits to the Adventurer's Guild in the past, most members, despite the guild's name, seldom actually traveled beyond the walls of Serpent's Keep. What tales were to be heard were often wild rumors with little fact underlying them, or were oft-repeated stories of adventures from long ago.

In the end, Jake left the Guild with no more than he had going in.

He did have an idea forming in the back of his mind that he would need to think on further... something born from his earlier journeys into the Outland. It wasn't much, but it was all he had. With nothing else to go on, it was better than waiting around for something to happen.

He was pulled abruptly from his thoughts when someone called out to him.

"Young Quigley." A small, thin, graying man crossed the street. Jake recognized him.

"Mason, isn't it?" Jake had crossed paths with Mason before. The man hadn't seemed to be quite all there the last time they had spoken, but several of Mason's observations had suggested that he may see more than folks gave him credit for.

"A brief word, if that's all right, Mister Quigley."

"Of course." Jake looked wistfully down the pedestrian thoroughfare in the direction of home. He started walking, leaving Mason to fall in line beside him. They passed a few villagers who were out and about; the lamp lighter continued to work his way down the street.

"You are recently returned, I understand," said Mason.

"That's right," Jake said cautiously. The last time they had spoken, Mason had scolded him for taking Meara into the Outland. He wondered what he could possibly have done wrong now.

"You traveled the threads with Master Tobias."

"That's right." He wondered at Mason using the term *threads*. Jake had found that it was the way the Jahai usually referred to the passages, both primary and side. His uncle Tobias used the term.

"And what be your plans now, young Quigley?"

"Pardon my bluntness, Mason, but how is it any of your concern?"

"I only be concerned for your well-being, sir." Mason stopped, reached out and took Jake by the arm. "There be wrong out there. Things be very wrong."

"What do you mean?" asked Jake.

Mason studied Jake's face. He saw something there.

"You saw it, I bet," said Mason. "You be a witness, I bet."

"What do you know of it?" asked Jake. Could Mason know something of what had happened, of how he had been separated from Tobias? How he had ended up at the steps of the Temple?

"There be cracks in the world, Jacob Quigley," said Mason.

"How so?"

"You've seen it. Things ain't right, and they be gettin' worse." He placed a hand on Jake's chest. "You know what I say be true. I sense it in you."

Jake took hold of Mason's wrist and pulled his hand away.

"What do you want, Mason?"

"You have to fix it, Quigley. You have to fix the world."

"Yeah? And how do I do that?"

"That be your path, sir."

"Right. Thanks for that," Jake frowned. For just a moment, he had thought this crazy old man knew something. "And what about your concern for my well-being?"

"It is your spirit that is in the shadows, my friend."

Standing in the mansion's main foyer, Jake took a moment and let the evening quiet of the house work to soothe him. Mrs. Hodges had no doubt gone home soon after dinner, and Mr. Griffin was probably settled into his room. He had a small suite just off the foyer to the left of the staircase.

Jake took the stairs to the second floor. His exchange with Mason had left him unsettled and he wasn't ready to go to his room. He instead continued on down the hall and stepped out onto the second floor deck. It opened out to the west, providing a scene of the village below, the west wall, and the Outland beyond the wall. Night had come. The criss-cross of streets within the village glowed with the street lamps and curtained lit windows.

A minute later Mr. Griffin came out onto the deck behind Jake. He hesitated briefly before stepping up beside him. He stood silent, noting that Jake was lost in thought.

"Good evening, Mr. Griffin," Jake said at last. He continued looking out past the village to the dark, heavily shadowed Outland beyond the wall.

"Good evening, Master Jacob." Griffin had heard Jake come into the mansion and had followed after him when he realized that Jake hadn't gone to his room.

"It's nice out," said Jake.

"It is."

They both stood quietly taking in the evening for some time.

"I missed this," Jake said finally.

"Yes, sir." Mr. Griffin paused a moment. "You'll be leaving, then."

Jake grinned at that. Nothing got by good ol' Griff. "Day after tomorrow."

"I see."

"I have to get supplies together."

There was another long pause. Mr. Griffin let out a calm sigh.

"Mrs. Hodges observed that you didn't eat much of your dinner before going out," he said. "She prepared a snack for you before leaving for the evening. It's waiting for you in the ice box."

Jake spent the next morning gathering supplies, including rations of dried fruit, cheese and bread, jerky. He also allowed himself some fresh vegetables.

Returning to the hidden command center off the mansion library, he packed an essentials kit, a first aid kit, and some extra clothes. He included the maps that he had drawn during his previous journeys into the Outland before shutting down the gate.

With everything ready to go, he stowed his gear and headed out of the command center. Coming into the library through the hidden panel, he found Meara sitting in one of the two chairs, waiting for him. She stood and put on an awkward grin.

"Where are we headed, Master Jacob?"

"Meara?" Jake closed the panel and stepped into the middle of the room. He was about to give her a hug but stopped short. Mr. Griffin had long ago made clear the separation between the master of the estate and staff.

"Yes, sir," said Meara. "It's great to see you."

"It's good to be back," said Jake. "I heard you were out at the Farm."

"That I was. I came back as soon as I got word." Meara's smile broadened. "So, when do we leave?"

"We?"

"You don't expect to do this all by yourself, do you, sir?"

Jake sat on the edge of the other chair, waiting for her to return to her seat.

"You don't even know what *this* is," he said then.

"To find Master Quigley, of course."

"That's the goal, yes, but—"

"That's good enough for me, sir."

"I see." Jake sat back, looked over at Meara. To be honest, he would feel better with her along. He may have more experience in the threads, but she was still the expert when it came to the dangers of the Outland. "We're heading for the Ravine."

"The Great Ravine?" Meara sounded genuinely surprised. "You mean, with the flying dragons?"

"It's the only place in the Outland that I know of where I can see something of the Other Worlds without having to step through a portal. We saw dragons there, and dragons aren't from around here."

"Right, sir." Meara managed a grin. "It should be fun."

Tobias moved off the trail and entered a wide clearing. The sun had set half an hour earlier and night would come soon to the Outland. He surveyed the shadows that were closing in on the clearing as he tossed his backpack aside. Satisfied that nothing was lying in wait for him, he began gathering dry branches and twigs from the surrounding forest. Once he had a small campfire going, he brought out the makings of his dinner. It would be a simple meal of soup and bread; what he really wanted was a cup of coffee.

Minutes later, sitting before the fire with coffee in hand and soup heating, Tobias felt an uncomfortable tingling throughout his body; the sensation of cobwebs brushing across his face, his arms. He lifted his gaze, looked across the clearing into the shadows of the surrounding woods.

Nothing...

Whatever it was, it wasn't coming from there.

Tobias set his cup down and stood up. He turned from the fire, looked about in all directions. He glanced up at the sky then. It was gray and growing darker.

But there was something odd about it. The color was... wrong. It was hard, like a shell. It sat over the world like a metallic dome, shining smooth.

Tobias moved out of the clearing and out onto the trail. He looked in both directions, then let his gaze slide slowly back to the sky. The color tinted the world. A heavy, hollow silence pushed in on him.

The world about him exploded then in shattering bright blue, a thousand cracks spiderwebbing across the dome; the landscape around Tobias burst blue and white, all shadows vanishing and revealing the underworld of the forest floor.

The white rushed in on Tobias, and in that white were flashes of images of people and places and landscapes, images from many worlds bleeding into this one.

And then it was gone. The bright was pushed back as shadows rushed back out from the surrounding forest, eating the white and the blue, snaking in and around trees and bushes; gray splashed across the sky.

The world was as it had been, with dusk quickly giving way to dark.

Tobias looked again up the trail, turned and looked down-trail. He looked up at the sky. The first stars were already beginning to show. He looked off-trail, back into the clearing. The flames of his small campfire flickered and danced.

Expect the soup is about ready...

Chapter Four

Mrs. Hodges stepped out of her booth and into the short back alley, bringing her wire basket cart out with her. Hers was the only booth in the alley, which ran behind several of the public booths up in the market plaza proper.

She slid the wood panels of her booth closed, set and clicked the padlock, then took the several steps up to the narrow access door that opened to the marketplace.

It was mid-afternoon, and there were only a handful of customers wandering from booth to booth. Mrs. Hodges started in the direction of the farmstand at the far end of the plaza. She needed to be home in time to prepare supper, though once again she would be cooking only for herself and Mr. Griffin.

She was worried about young Master Jacob; home only a few days and now off again, no doubt getting himself into all sorts of trouble. The boy was very much like Master Quigley, continually facing down danger in one righteous cause after another.

She stopped briefly at Mrs. Numidia's booth along the way. Her friend sold tools and other items handmade by her husband, the village blacksmith. Mrs. Hodges seldom had need for such items, but the two women got along well and Mrs. Hodges' less than reputable herbalist activities had never bothered Mrs. Numidia the way it did some of the other villagers.

She excused herself after a few minutes and continued on to the farmstand. The man behind the counter had returned from the farm with Meara, and so considered himself on the inside regarding all the news of Jacob Quigley. Mrs. Hodges smiled patiently and nodded at all the right times, managed finally to break away after purchasing several days' worth of fruit and vegetables.

She passed Mrs. Gyles' booth on the way out. She had hoped for a brief word with Meara's mother, but the booth was already shut down for the day. She continued on out of the marketplace and moved out into the main thoroughfare.

Walking through the village, she met Mr. Dante as he was coming out of his bank. He was on his way to an afternoon meeting with a young man seeking a business loan. They were getting together at the café for coffee.

The café was just about a second home to Mr. Dante.

Mrs. Hodges was about to comment on what she believed to be the young man's considerable integrity when the sky overhead suddenly turned a bright, explosive blue, sending Mr. Dante's face aglow. It lasted only a moment, and then all was back to normal.

"Oh my," said Mr. Dante. "Peculiar weather we've been having these past few days; eh, Mrs. Hodges?"

"Strange indeed," Mrs. Hodges said warily. This wasn't right, and it had nothing to do with weather.

Mr. Dante managed an uncomfortable smile.

"On my way, then." He gave a slight bow of the head. "Please give Mr. Griffin my best."

"I will, Mr. Dante," said Mrs. Hodges. "I certainly will."

Mr. Dante hurried on, leaving Mrs. Hodges to follow along after, pulling her wire basket cart behind her. She only managed another dozen steps when she heard someone call her name. She stopped and looked behind her.

"Hello, Mason," she said.

Mason looked anxious; not unusual for Mason.

"Mrs. Hodges."

"Is everything all right? You appear troubled."

"That I am, ma'am. A bit and then some."

"Is that so?" They started walking, Mrs. Hodges pulling her cart behind her.

She and Mason had been friends for more than thirty years. They had never moved in the same circles, and Mason had found himself isolated from most in the village these past years, but Mrs. Hodges and Mason had a shared history. They often passed the time in pleasant conversation.

"Did you see what happened a few minutes ago?" he asked.

"I did. Would you know what that was?"

"It's a sign," said Mason.

"How so?" Mrs. Hodges stopped and turned to look directly at Mason. Something had him rattled. "A sign of what?"

"Young Jacob didn't heed my warning. Now I fear the worst."

"In what way?" asked Mrs. Hodges. "We've talked about this before, Mason. You're not making yourself clear."

Mason grumbled to himself. He knew that much of his awkwardness with his fellow villagers was due to his inability to clearly articulate his thoughts.

He had spent so many years alone.

"There's bad happening in the passageways, ma'am," he said.

"The passageways are closed," Mrs. Hodges stated flatly. "Jacob closed them when he shut down Serpent's Gate."

"The gates are closed, that's for true, but there's threads seeking worlds, more and more by the day."

"How that can be?" asked Mrs. Hodges. "Mason, passageways can't exist without gates. Even side passages need landings."

"There be a power out there, Mrs. Hodges. I see it. There be cracks in the world. I don't know how or why, but I can see it. You know me. You see I speak true."

Mrs. Hodges did at that. Mason saw things, felt things, sensed things. The problem was, his visions often meant something wildly different than what he saw. They may be based on reality, but not necessarily his reality.

This time out however, it seemed clear. Whatever may be causing it, there was *bad happening in the passageways.*

From the signs, the village itself might be in danger; perhaps the world.

Mrs. Hodges placed a comforting hand on Mason's arm. "We'll just have to trust in Master Jacob, Mason. There's not much else we can do, so far as I can see."

Mason wasn't much comforted by that.

"Cracks in the world, ma'am," he stated firmly. "Bad happenings. Bad, bad happenings."

Jake and Meara were sitting near their campfire, their gear stacked nearby. The flames from the fire sent shadows dancing across their faces, and behind them, across the wall of trees that surrounded the small clearing. They had finished their evening meal and sat silent now with cups of coffee in hand.

They had followed Jake's hand drawn maps since leaving Serpent's Keep, and by his reckoning they were about a day from the Great Ravine. The journey had so far been uneventful.

Meara broke the silence and asked not for the first time about Jake's time *out there*, after he had closed the gate. Jake hadn't spoken very much about his experiences in the passageways, the *'threads'* as Tobias often referred to them, the name the Jahai used. He had told her of finding Tobias, of their escape from the landing once a thread had unexpectedly formed, but little else. Now, as he stared into the glowing embers of the campfire, he found himself drawn back there, to those ethereal threads.

"We moved from landing to landing," he said distantly. "We never knew where we were going to end up, nothing being what it should be. Threads appeared and vanished. Some of the worlds were incredible, but most were empty."

"Were any of them like the Other Worlds we went to?"

"No," he sighed. "Nothing like those."

The Other Worlds had been variations of their own world. The landings that Jake and Tobias had visited while trapped in the side passages had for the most part been unearthly, in many ways unreal. Only occasionally had they found themselves on a world that was in any way familiar, and where they could replenish supplies.

Jake looked up from the fire, which was slowly dying down to glowing coals. He took a swallow of his coffee, looked at Meara. "So... how did _you_ spend the last seven months?"

"Me?" Meara gave a tired shrug. "I dusted furniture, swept floors; picked vegetables... scary times."

"Sounds like it," said Jake, trying a thin smile. He took a last swallow of his coffee. "We'll be at the ravine tomorrow, another day to get to the entrance."

"Should be fun, sir."

"It could be quite a letdown for you, after picking tomatoes."

"I'll try not to expect too much, sir."

It was late; the world was quiet, the Quigley Estate asleep. Tobias was in the kitchen, sitting at the island counter eating a sandwich. A nearby oil lamp provided the only light.

He sensed movement in the shadow of the open doorway leading to the rest of the house. He took a bite of his sandwich, spoke without looking up.

"We're running low on mustard." He set his sandwich down on the plate and took a long drink from his glass of milk. "And milk."

Mr. Griffin wasn't sure how to respond.

"I'll let Mrs. Hodges know, sir."

Tobias picked up his sandwich then and took another bite. "Are you hungry?" he asked. "I'll make you a sandwich."

"No sir. Thank you." Mr. Griffin stepped fully into the kitchen. He was carrying a small club. "I heard noises; I came to check."

"Good man." Tobias finished his sandwich. He took another drink of his milk, looked over the rim of the glass at Mr. Griffin. The man hadn't changed at all. "I missed you, Griffin. Can't tell you how much I've missed you."

"Yes sir." Mr. Griffin leaned the club against the wall and took another step nearer the counter. "It is very good to see you, Master Quigley."

"You too, my dear friend." Tobias finished his milk, set aside his glass and plate. "I don't suppose you've seen my nephew?"

"Come and gone, sir. Looking for you."

"Is that so?"

"I believe he's headed for the Great Ravine."

"Of course," Tobias grumbled. He rested his arms on the counter, clasped his hands and frowned. Deep lines formed on his forehead.

"Is everything all right, sir?" asked Mr. Griffin.

Tobias had traveled first to the Temple, gotten news on young Jacob before returning to Serpent's Keep. Maybe if he had come straight to the village, as he had first considered...

"One of us is going to have to stop and let the other catch up," he said.

Chapter Five

Jake and Meara reached the wide ledge overlooking the Great Ravine in the late afternoon, shortly before dusk. The ravine was hundreds of yards across, a thousand yards deep, and ran east and west as far as the eye could see. The walls of the ravine were steep and the floor was hidden beneath a canopy of dark forest and darker undergrowth. At this time of the day there was no sign of the flying dragons that Jake knew to inhabit the Great Ravine.

There was a circle of stones near the back of the ledge, evidence of Jake and Meara's campsite from their previous visit there. Meara set about making the fire pit ready as Jake searched the perimeter for kindling and firewood. Once they were settled in, with their camp organized, they returned to the edge of the precipice and waited.

Come the dusk and the quickly darkening gray of the ravine, they began to see shadows skimming above the canopy below. Large, black silhouettes, gliding silently, created darker shadows that danced in the treetops beneath them. There were only a few at first, but as they watched another and then another appeared, dragons coming out of their cliff-wall dwellings to fly above the black forest of the chasm.

Jake and Meara watched until it was too dark to see, then returned to their campfire near the back of the ledge. They ate a light dinner and then settled in for an early night, wanting to get an early start the next morning.

They left the ledge just after dawn, as soon as it was light enough that they could see where they were walking. They followed along the edge of the ravine for most of the morning before the terrain forced them to move into the woods. Without a trail, they continued downslope, eventually finding an animal trail that wound through the thick undergrowth and eventually brought them again to the ravine's edge. The chasm was much shallower here, at most a third as deep as further up-ravine, and the forest canopy that hid the ravine floor was much closer.

Continuing east, the trail they followed led them steadily downhill, the ravine growing steadily shallower, the forest-covered floor seeming to rise up to meet them. They came out into a wide clearing in late afternoon.

The mouth of the ravine was on their left, half-hidden behind a wall of tall, thick brush. A large stone, five feet high, irregularly shaped, four feet wide at its widest, stood in the center of the clearing. It had at one time been the pylon that when opened had become the gateway to one of the Other Worlds.

Now it was just a stone.

Jake couldn't help but reach out and lay a hand on the granite. It was cool to the touch.

Meara watched from a distance.

"Memories, Master Jacob?" she asked.

"You could say that."

Meara looked in the direction of the mouth of the Great Ravine. A dragon had come out of there the last time they were here.

"Me too," she said, hardly more than a whisper.

Jake turned from the stone. "What say we make camp, start into the ravine in the morning?"

§

The great trees were spaced dozens of feet apart, many of the massive trunks eight to ten feet in diameter. The thick green canopy overhead nearly blotted out the sky, creating a permanent twilight beneath. The floor of the ravine was deep with mulch from centuries of falling needles and decayed branches. The only undergrowth was the occasional giant fern or cluster of salal, leaving much of the forest floor open.

Jake and Meara travelled up the heart of the ravine throughout the morning, with only the sound of their breathing and their muffled footfalls breaking the ominous, heavy silence of the forest. Despite the ravine being in his own world, in his own time, Jake thought it an alien place, more alien than any world he had visited since first arriving at Serpent's Keep and beginning his quest... now so very long ago.

They came upon a small brook at what Jake guessed to be about midday. They stopped, filled their canteens and ate from their rations. As they rested on the bank, filtered streaks of sunlight reached down to them through the canopy, creating sparkles of glitter on the surface of the meandering stream as it slowly worked its way past them.

"It's so quiet here," said Meara, not for the first time. "Not just quiet. It feels empty."

"At least we don't have to worry about wolves or bandits," said Jake. They had experienced both during their travels in the Outland the previous year.

"Then why don't I feel any safer?"

"I can't imagine." Jake looked calmly about them, into the shadows of a forest like he had never seen before. The quiet wasn't absolute. There was the hollow rippling sound of the brook, but that somehow made the enveloping silence all the more ominous.

He straightened and prepared to stand. "We should get at it. Best we get wherever we're going before it gets dark."

"How much darker can it get?" mumbled Meara.

"I'm guessing quite a lot."

They slipped back into their backpacks and started out again. They followed the stream until they found a narrow spot to cross. Several hours later the forest ahead shone just a little brighter. Drawing nearer, they could see that the trees here stood further apart.

They stepped out into a large clearing.

It wasn't completely open overhead, but the canopy was much thinner here, letting in what light there was. Evening wasn't far off, and the sky was already beginning to gray. Jake could just make out the dark mouths of caves set into the sheer walls of the ravine rising up to the sky.

Directly ahead, three dragons sat on a row of short pillars; flying dragons, their wings tucked back along their sides. The one in the center raised its head up and back, then forward, all while watching the two humans step into the center of the clearing.

Only when Jake and Meara were within easy conversation distance did it speak.

"You are welcome here, Jake, blood of Tobias."

Jake stopped two paces from the dragons, Meara beside him.

"You were expecting us?"

"Know you," the dragon said haltingly. "Watch you come here."

Jake looked back the way they had come, traveling up the ravine from the canyon mouth. He turned his attention back to the dragons. The two sitting to either side remained silent, though attentive. The dragon in the center appeared to be the leader and the speaker of the group.

"You better now," it stated very matter-of-factly.

Better now? What did he mean by that? Did these dragons know something? Did they know anything about how Jake ended up at the steps of the temple?

"Um... yes. I am; much better." Jake took another half-step toward the line of dragons. "Do you know of when I was *not* better?"

"Yes." There was a change in the dragon's expression, but Jake couldn't tell what it was or what it might mean. He knew from his previous encounters that all the dragon species were very intelligent, but that many were limited in how they could express themselves and how their emotions were reflected on their faces.

If they knew what happened to Jake, might they know what happened to Uncle Tobias?

Tobias was much better at understanding and reading the dragons than Jake, but then Tobias had spent a lifetime with them. If only he was here now...

"Have you seen my uncle?" he asked. "Tobias Quigley. Is he... *better?*"

"Tobias Quigley not hurt."

Okay. That sounds promising...

"Do you know where he is?"

"You better now. You fix."

"Fix? Fix what?"

"Threads bad. You fix threads."

Meara leaned nearer to Jake. "What does he mean? *Threads?*"

"The passageways," said Jake. "The dragons call them threads."

"Yes," said the dragon. Dragons had keen hearing. "You fix threads."

Dragons were always asking him to fix things.

"Okay. I will," said Jake. "But first I need to find Tobias. I find Tobias, together we'll fix the threads."

The dragon lifted his head high, looked down at the two humans. His expression changed yet again. It might have been humor; a smile or a smirk.

"So said Tobias Quigley," said the dragon.

Tobias held the small backpack open on the stool and began transferring food and other supplies from the kitchen's island counter into the pack. It was an hour before dawn, and he planned to leave Serpent's Keep well before the sun came up.

Mrs. Hodges was standing on the other side of the counter. She was wrapping a brick of cheese in a cloth. "It's a shame you can't spend a few more days with us, Master Quigley."

"I feel the same, Mrs. Hodges," said Tobias. "I do so miss our evenings at the card table."

"Canasta just isn't the same without you."

"I promise a long stay at home once we get back, dear lady."

"I look forward to that." Mrs. Hodges handed him the wrapped block of cheese. She wore a thoughtful smile. "You know, sir, young Jacob isn't all that different from you; when you were his age."

Tobias finished packing, began tying down the straps. "My memory has a hard time reaching that far back, Mrs. Hodges."

"I don't believe that for a second." Her warm smile faded. "You be careful, sir. You and the boy, both."

"That we shall, Mrs. Hodges." Tobias lifted the pack and slipped an arm into one shoulder strap. He held the other arm out across the counter and took Mrs. Hodges by the hand. "I'll be back before you know it."

Janice walked across the rooftop deck through a network of walkways and raised garden beds; she stood at the very edge. The building reached hundreds of feet up from an empty, desolate plain below into a metallic-orange sky that hovered over this strange world. She lifted her gaze outward, pushed her thin frame against a stiff breeze. She appeared as a well-kept middle-aged woman, a smooth complexion but for the slightest onset of wrinkles at the corners of her sharp blue eyes. Her hair was full, fell to her shoulders, brushed back now by the wind.

She lifted a hand and pushed it out against the scene before her. This world before her was hers; all hers, to do with what she would.

Her image flickered briefly, as if shifting out of and back into existence. She lowered her hand, paused; she waited; her form solidified. She raised her hand again, hesitated... she rubbed her fingertips together. In the distance, near the horizon beyond the plain, there came explosions of light and color; silent flashes, as of cracks in the universe.

Another flash then, blinding, erasing the sky and the plain and the rooftop deck.

Janice was strapped in a standing frame, her eyes closed. Wires and plugs were attached to her head and her arms. Her expression was terse, her countenance tense. She appeared older, grayer, more weathered than the Janice on the rooftop. There was darkness in her countenance, an emotional shadow over her face, and when she opened her eyes there was intensity, resolve.

Her assistant stood at the monitoring station beside the standing frame. Martin was a short, squat man with disheveled hair and ill-fitting clothes. He pressed several keys on the monitor's keypanel, turned to Janice and began disconnecting her from the equipment.

"It went well?" he asked, setting the lines onto a nearby tray.

"It did not," said Janice. Her words were cold. She stepped out of the standing frame. "We'll have to reset and try again."

"The location was very precise," said Martin.

"Perhaps, but something went wrong. I could feel it from the start." She looked sharply at her assistant. "I slipped out for a moment. It was all I could do to maintain presence."

"How is that possible? Janice, the plane emanates from you."

"I know that, Martin," she said icily. "I created it."

"Of course," said Martin, bowing his head. He stepped aside and Janice moved to the monitor. She began reviewing the data, and after several moments brought up a code window.

It had taken her years to get free from the landing that Tobias had trapped her in, recreating from scratch an access to the ancillary threads. Since then she had worked unceasing to find a way out of the secondary planes and back to primary. This work had involved the repurposing of numerous secondary and tertiary threads. None had as yet given her access to the primary web.

She was certain that she was getting close. A number of the threads had actually breached the primary web, if only for a fraction of a second. These had caused some disruptions in the web, and on occasion had generated fractures, some of which yet remained.

Nonetheless, this gave her optimism. Success would come.

For the moment, she remained trapped in these infuriatingly restrictive side passages and landings. But once she reached the primary web, she would find her way to Serpent's Gate. Once she had access to that, the Rhetani would spread truth and stability across the universe.

And Tobias would be unable to stop them.

Chapter Six

Jake and Meara were escorted to a small encampment a short distance from the main clearing. There were several small structures, obviously made for human use, and a permanent campfire pit. A small supply of firewood was stacked nearby.

The dragon that had guided them there told them that one of the structures was for sleeping, another contained supplies. They were free to replenish their own supplies as needed. If they chose to start a fire for cooking or warmth, they should keep it small.

The dragon informed them that they would be escorted back to the main plaza in the morning and then left the two humans to their evening.

The sun had set sometime earlier, and it would be fully dark soon. Meara began building a fire as Jake explored the dwellings. By the time he returned to Meara, she had the fire going.

"What now?" she asked.

"We have something to eat and then get a good night's sleep. I guess we're out again in the morning."

"To this Village of the Dragons?"

It had been suggested they go there to wait for Tobias, after which together they would 'fix the threads'.

"It looks that way," said Jake. "And I can't think of a better option."

"We could stay here."

Jake knelt before the fire, nodded in the direction of the plaza. "They seem pretty keen on sending us to this village of theirs."

Jake had never been to the Village of the Dragons, though Tobias had mentioned it in passing once or twice. If he understood correctly, it served as a sort of hub for a handful of side passages within the web. It had been stable until recently. But according to the dragons, a number of new, not so stable threads had formed and attached to the village. This was causing disruption everywhere.

Which was why Meara wasn't completely sold on the idea of taking a thread there.

"It'll be fine, Meara," said Jake.

"Right," grumbled Meara.

"I'm sure it'll be fine. Really. They wouldn't send us through if they didn't think it would be fine."

"Right," she said again.

They fell silent, spoke only sporadically as they prepared and then ate dinner. Afterward, they spent some time sitting quietly at the fire before settling in for the night.

The dragon returned in the morning and they were escorted back to the main clearing. Dragons didn't appear to be all that big on the concept of mornings, and there were only a handful of them about. One stood at the edge of the clearing near a raised dais and was waiting for them. Their escort moved to one side as Jake and Meara approached.

On the dais sat the small passage stone.

"Safe journey," said the dragon. "You are expected."

"Yes," said Jake. "Thanks."

"Right," said Meara.

The dragon moved further aside and waited. Jake took Meara's hand, gave her a playful wink. He reached out and placed his free hand on the stone.

They were enveloped in the familiar empty white, awash in light and the onrush of warped space. It lasted for several seconds, and they stumbled out on the other side.

They found themselves standing inside a circular room. Behind them stood a circle of six daises similar to the one they had just left. The floor was dirt; there was no furniture, there were no windows and only one tall, wide opening that would be large enough for the largest of dragons.

"See," said Jake. "No problem."

"Uh, huh."

They approached the opening and stepped outside. A pair of Thrauhm dragons stood watch to either side of the opening. Both glanced down at the two humans without turning their heads. One gave a slight welcoming nod.

"See? We're expected," mumbled Jake to Meara.

"Uh, huh," said Meara.

They were looking out across the open central plaza of a sprawling village. All along the perimeter of the community were large, stark cavernous structures set in amongst the enclosing forest. To Jake's left was a building that was much larger and more substantial than the others.

A number of dragons from many different species were moving about the Village of the Dragons. One of the Bentai species stood a few yards in front of the new arrivals, watching patiently, his hands clasped in front of him. He bowed his head and raised it again.

"Welcome Jake, blood of Tobias." He then acknowledged Meara, "Welcome, companion of Jake."

"Meara," Meara said coolly.

"You are welcome here, Meara."

"Thanks." Meara had never seen a Bentai. They were eerily humanoid in appearance. She was a bit taken aback.

"I am Khol. I speak for Natan, leader of the Jahai. He wishes you to be comfortable during your stay."

"Thank you, Khol." Jake looked around the plaza. Several of the dragons milling about were looking back at the two humans. "I don't suppose Tobias is here."

"He was with us only days past; not now." He turned and started across the plaza, walking in the direction of a small structure with a human-sized door and two small windows. He was clearly expecting them to follow. "We hope this dwelling suits your needs. It is similar to dwellings for Tobias Quigley."

"I'm sure it will be fine."

Khol indicated a box sitting on the ground beside the door. "We have provided food for humans."

"Thank you."

"Do you expect Master Quigley soon?" asked Meara.

"I cannot say. We have sent word out that you will be here."

Two days later, in early midmorning, Jake was escorted to the Grand Hall for an audience with Natan. Entering the chamber and approaching the raised wooden throne platform, he was surprised to find Tobias standing before the Jahai leader. He had heard nothing of his uncle arriving in the Village of the Dragons.

Tobias gave Jake a simple hello nod as his nephew stepped up beside him. He turned his attention to the leader of the Jahai.

"My friend Natan, I introduce Jacob Quigley, my nephew."

Natan silently acknowledged the introduction as he studied the young human Jake.

"You are welcome here, Jacob Quigley, nephew of our friend Tobias Quigley."

"Thank you," said Jake. "I am honored to be here."

"Yes." Natan turned his attention back to Tobias. "The journey that you would undertake is a dangerous one, our friend. But I agree. It may be the best of the few options that are available to you."

"The greater the chance for success with my nephew as traveling companion. With your permission, we will depart in the morning."

Natan turned again to Jake. "Words of your deed have reached this hall, Jacob Quigley," he said. "Tobias is wise to seek your companionship. You will attend him."

"Of course."

Natan turned a final time to Tobias. "Success to you, our friend Tobias Quigley."

"Thank you, friend Natan. We will seek an audience upon our return." Tobias stepped back, turned about and started away from the throne. Jake gave several uncertain nods to Natan and quickly followed after his uncle.

Stepping outside, he stood next to Tobias.

"It is good to see you, uncle," he said.

"And you, nephew." Tobias started across the open plaza. "You and Meara are staying in the huts?"

"It is where they put us." Jake stepped in line and they continued across the square. Tobias made a halfhearted attempt at conversation about the two of them getting separated, about following after one another. He told Jake that Mrs. Hodges sent her best.

His mind seemed to be elsewhere.

Meara was sitting at the campfire outside the huts. She stood when they approached.

"Master Tobias!"

"Meara, my dear." Tobias reached out and warmly took Meara's hand in both of his. He reached out then and pulled her close, gave her a warm hug.

What would Mr. Griffin have to say about that?

"Tobias, what's this journey we're going on?" Jake asked.

"Yes, yes... to it, then." Tobias indicated the short wooden stools of the permanent campsite. He sat and they sat opposite the small fire from him. "We are going to see the Ancient Guardian."

"Okay. And just who, or what, is the Ancient Guardian?"

"He was the first of us, as his title would suggest."

The first of us... Jake had never thought of Tobias as one of the guardians. He had just assumed that role fell to the Jahai dragons.

"He sounds like quite the fellow," said Jake.

"Rather," said Tobias. "It was while on my way here that I realized a visit to the Ancient Guardian may be the only way to resolve our dilemma."

"Your pal Janice does seem to be advancing her plans apace."

"So you've noticed."

"We have."

"And this Ancient Guardian can fix things?" asked Meara.

"I am hoping that at the very least he will be able to point us in the right direction," said Tobias. "It is believed that he was responsible for the gateways and the web underlying it all."

"That's good enough for me, sir," said Meara.

"Um..." Jake held up a hand, raised a finger. "Uncle Tobias? Your friend back there; Natan. He hinted as to possible danger on this journey."

"Quite so." Tobias gave a long, loud sigh. "To reach the Ancient Guardian, we must travel what the Jahai refer to as the Dark Path."

"The Dark Path..."

"So it is called."

"And it is dangerous?" asked Meara.

"So it is said," shrugged Tobias. "Not the word I would use."

Chapter Seven

Khol led them out of the Village of the Dragons just after dawn, their departure witnessed by a handful of solemn Jahai, the majority of the village residents still asleep. They followed a wide but little-used path away from the village; Jake saw that some of the branches of the encroaching vegetation had recently been cut back. After several hundred yards, they came upon a tall, wooden double-gate that blocked the trail. A weathered fence stretched away from the gate in both directions, disappearing into the brush on either side.

Khol stepped off the trail beside the gate and waited.

"What now?" asked Meara, to no one in particular.

"So it begins," said Tobias.

"The Dark Path? Here?"

"Successful journey to you," Khol gave a slow nod. "I can go no further."

"We thank you for your help, friend Khol," said Tobias.

The Jahai dragon gave another curt nod in response, stepped back another step and again waited.

"And so." Tobias looked to Jake and Meara. "Shall we?" indicating the gate.

"Right, sir," said Meara.

"Ready when you are, uncle," said Jake.

"Lead on, then," Tobias urged.

Jake stepped forward and lifted the wooden crossbar. He pushed the gate inward and walked through. Meara followed.

Tobias turned to Khol. "We will see you upon our return."

"One will stand watch awaiting that return, our friend Tobias Quigley."

Tobias followed the others through the gate. It closed slowly behind him; came the sound of the crossbar sliding back into position.

The trail ahead quickly narrowed; the brush on either side was tall and full, the forest beyond the brush stood dark and eerily quiet. The gray sky overhead lay heavy over the landscape.

The three walked single file, Tobias moving out ahead and leading the way.

"What now, Tobias?" asked Jake. "How far to this Ancient Guardian?"

Tobias shrugged a shoulder as he walked. "I haven't a clue, dear boy; I've never been here before."

"But I thought... what you said... I thought you'd met this guardian."

"Oh yes." There was the hint of something more, but Tobias left it unsaid. He looked briefly back at Jake. "We have not spoken since he took up residence here."

"Sir?" Meara piped up from the end of the line. "We don't know what's ahead?"

"That's nothing new for us, Meara," said Jake. "When have we ever known what we were walking into?"

The gateways... the Other Worlds...

"That's certainly true enough," said Meara.

"I'm afraid I don't know anyone who has gone through the gate," said Tobias. "But there are said to be several, shall we say, *situations...* between the gate and where the Ancient Guardian dwells. However, despite what Natan alluded, there is nothing to say there is actual danger involved."

Jake looked back to Meara. "See? Just like old times."

Tobias couldn't help but offer a final observation. "Then, there is nothing to say there is not."

Meara tried to sound upbeat. "It should be fun, sir."

Three quarters of an hour passed in relative silence, with only the occasional comment about a gray sky that only slightly lightened, or the dampness of the encroaching vegetation that threatened to swallow up the trail.

Coming around a bend in the trail then, they approached a primitive milestone marker that was set alongside the trail. The stone was about a foot tall, and while there were no markings on its face, it nonetheless didn't look natural. It had the look of having been shaped, albeit a very long time ago.

Further up the trail, a few yards beyond the milestone, a faint shimmer lay across the path, as of a micro-thin sheet of water being brushed by a faint breeze.

"What's that?" asked Meara.

"Well, well," Tobias stated matter-of-factly. He stepped forward past the milestone. He stopped a pace before the barrier, reached out and lightly tapped at it with two fingers. There didn't look to be any reaction. He studied his fingers, rubbed the tips with his thumb.

He looked back to Jake and Meara. He gave a wink and a slight smile. He turned forward and stepped calmly through the shimmering wall. He continued another two steps, stopped.

He looked about briefly, then waved for the others to come through.

Jake didn't feel anything as he walked through, not as he had when he traveled the gateways. Once on the other side, however, he noted a change in the air; it felt slightly warmer and dryer. And the smell was different; less musty, less mulchy.

But the main difference he noted was the view before them. They definitely were not where they had been a few steps back.

The forest ahead thinned, with the trail opening out to a wide expanse of low, grassy hillocks with occasional clusters of squat trees; here and there were narrow bands of brush that likely followed rivers or streams.

And beyond the plain, a castle was just visible set midway up a steep mountainside. The stone walls of the structure were as dark as the mountain itself.

"My friends," said Tobias. "I believe that is where we need to go."

"Looks simple enough, sir," said Meara.

Jake sighed doubtfully. "I'm thinking not."

"Sir?"

"There are those '*situations*' that Uncle Tobias spoke of."

"Right," said Meara. "Those."

"Off we go then?" Tobias said brightly.

"Yes sir," Meara said tentatively.

"Lead on, uncle," said Jake.

They followed the trail out onto the plain and the rolling hills and started toward the mountain with the castle on the horizon. There was no wind, not the slightest breeze, and the eerie quiet of the forest they had left behind followed after them, surrounding them. Colors faded, leaving only varied shades of gray.

They traveled until the grays darkened and they sensed dusk was nearing. They made camp along the bank of a wide stream, collected dry branches and twigs from surrounding brush for their fire.

The mountain was a dark silhouette in the distance, disappearing into the black as night fell. Tobias, Jake and Meara sat close by the campfire. The crackling sound of burning branches echoed out into the darkness beyond the reach of the firelight.

Jake couldn't help but be reminded of his other travels across the landscapes of other worlds. How many times had he sat before a flickering campfire, under an Other World sky?

Surreal worlds with dragons flying overhead, dark silhouettes set against bright moons...

He looked up from the fire, looked in the direction of the castle set into the mountainside, hidden now in the dark.

"How can we be sure he's still there?" he asked, not so much a question as an observation.

Tobias glanced in the direction Jake was looking, turned back to the fire.

"I don't suppose we can," he said. "'cept, no reason to think he's not."

They reached the edge of a deep gulley and followed the worn trail that ran along the rim for most of the morning. Vegetation grew thicker here, even more so down in the gulley itself, which looked to be the remnant of a streambed or wash; Tobias suspected it may fill during a heavy rain.

The trail eventually veered away from the gulley, disappearing into tall scrub brush. As the trail continued the way they wanted to go, they followed it in.

Several dozen feet into the brush, the trail straightened and widened. Set alongside the trail was another milestone marker. The trail beyond the stone didn't look any different than the trail behind them; and while the marker looked much like the last one, there was nothing to indicate a barrier like the one they had passed through earlier. There was no shimmering, transparent wall; the terrain up-trail appeared normal.

Tobias moved ahead without saying a word. Jake looked back once at Meara, then followed after his uncle. He glanced at the marker as he passed it, took three steps further and stepped up beside Tobias.

He heard Meara come up behind them.

"Oh my," she said. The terrain had changed. They had definitely passed through a barrier.

The mountainside castle was still visible, but the landscape directly ahead was now foothills covered in tall yellow grass and scattered groves of old, gnarly oak trees. The sky was dark gray, and Jake couldn't tell if it was morning or afternoon.

Which made him wonder... *is the time of day here different than it was a minute ago?*

Tobias continued to lead the way forward. The path led directly to the first hill, then turned right and took the slope gradually up to the rise. They passed twisted, brownish gray trees, faded yellow grass and thorny bramble brush.

As they approached the ridge, they began to see the tops of what looked to be broken building spires rising up from the basin on the other side of the hill. Coming up over the top, the gentle downslope fell away to a thinly wooded forest of oak and alder and evergreen, looking much as the Outland they were familiar with. In the heart of the woods they could see the ruin of a cluster of interconnected-buildings, now little more than the jagged outlines of broken walls.

The trail they were on led switchback down the hillside and then straight to the ruin. As they drew nearer, they could see stone stairs leading up to what had no doubt at one time been double doors but was now an opening leading to a foyer with no ceiling or walls. The shard remains of tall, broken spires rose on either side of the stairs, now empty towers.

Meara climbed the stairs and stood in what remained of the door jamb.

"This looks a lot like..." she started thoughtfully.

"Like the Temple?" finished Jake.

"Like the Temple," finished Meara.

The similarity to the temple in the Outland near Serpent's Keep was striking. The basic design was evident here. The wall foundations, tower remnants, it was all here; including the surrounding landscape.

"Yes," said Tobias. There was a deeply melancholy look about him. He was clearly disturbed by the site of the temple ruins. "There were a number of temples, on a number of worlds."

"Uncle Tobias?" asked Jake. "Are you all right?"

"Of course, Jake." Tobias attempted a weak smile. "I was unaware that one such temple was here on the Dark Path."

It doesn't make sense...

"All right," Jake mumbled uncertainly. He looked about at the ruin. *What had happened here? Neglected, long ago abandoned? Or something more ominous?*

They left the stairs and walked cautiously among the ruin. There were rotted wooden beams among broken stone and chunks of concrete, rusted handmade nails, and not much else. Rooms and halls were identifiable by the wall foundations and the jagged gaps where windows once looked out on temple grounds. They could see where the monk sleeping cells had once lined narrow hallways.

The sound of scraping stone came from the other side of the broken wall ahead of them, rubble scrabbling onto the ground. A silhouette appeared above the top of the wall. A dragon settled there, looked calmly down at the three humans. It was of the sleek Lynhaur species; colored in multiple shades of green and brown, with powerful hind legs, slightly smaller front legs. Its leathery wings were folded back along its sides.

Tobias looked up at the dragon, studied it a moment, and finally smiled.

"Friend Lamal," he said. "What are you doing here on the Dark Path?"

"Tobias Quigley," said the dragon. Human speech did not come easily to Thrauhm dragons. Lamal shifted his position to gain a better perch on the wall. "Not Dark Path. Pelonar."

Tobias considered, hesitated. *This is the temple on Pelonar?*

"I see," he said, reflectively.

"Tobias?" asked Jake.

Tobias gave a thank you nod to Lamal, turned to Jake and Meara. "This temple ruin isn't on the Dark Path. We are on Pelonar."

"Yes, but..." Jake started, stopped. He thought back on their journey so far, the markers, the barriers. "I think I understand," he said.

"Yes?" Tobias asked.

"Yes."

"Well, I don't," said Meara. "At least I don't think I do."

Jake looked from Meara to Tobias. "If I have this right, the Dark Path is a single thread, but it passes through landings on a number of worlds."

"Precisely," said Tobias. "The thread itself exists on its own plane, and as we move along the path, we pass through each landing."

Meara indicated the mountain in the distance. She spoke to her understanding of what her companions were saying. "The Dark Path, and the castle, are on their own world," she said. "The landings are here, and yet they are not here. They sit along the thread."

"Exactly."

"And we see the castle whether we're on the Dark Path or in a landing?" There was some doubt in her tone.

"Um... yes. That's true. It is, after all, the Dark Path."

"Yes sir," said Meara. She was willing to accept the explanation because Tobias accepted it.

Tobias turned his attention back to the Jahai. "We journey the Dark Path, my friend. We would seek an audience with the Ancient Guardian."

"I have seen the shadows. You would undo what is being done."

"We are going to try, friend Lamal," said Tobias. He thought to himself... *we search for direction from the First of us.*

The Jahai looked away from Tobias, looked to Meara and Jake.

"I'm Jake," said Jake. How many dragons had he faced along his last quest? *I am blood of Tobias...*

"I know. Jake," said the dragon. "You help... *uncle.*"

I am blood of Tobias...

"That's me," said Jake.

"I'm Meara," Meara said snidely. She had also faced more than a few dragons. All in all, she thought they were very honorable; they were also more than a bit full of themselves.

"Meara," said the dragon. "Help Jake."

"Right."

The dragon let his gaze drift back to Tobias. It again shifted position, adjusted its perch on the top of the broken, jagged wall. Small bits of stone and gravel fell away as it settled back down.

"You pass now. You go," said the dragon. "Dark Path."

Chapter Eight

The castle was no longer visible through the tall trees of the sprawling forest they had entered hours earlier. Now working their way up steep terrain, the trail wound and switch-backed, the path occasionally so steep that Jake and the others were forced to grab onto exposed tree roots that grew across the trail in order to pull themselves up.

Clambering over yet another large root, they stepped out onto a level stretch of path. Sections of old wooden fencing lined one side of the trail. After a few dozen yards they came around a bend in the trail and up to another milestone marker.

Jake looked for some sign of a barrier across the trail. "I don't see anything."

"As before," said Tobias. "Onward, nephew."

Jake led the way, continuing past the marker. He sensed passing through the barrier, but didn't see much difference on the other side. The air was just as damp as before, and what sky he could see above the treetops was just as gray.

Once the others had come through the barrier, they continued up the trail. After a short distance it switch-backed and began to climb again. Another switchback and the trail leveled out.

Ahead, a small, rustic cabin was set along the side of the trail where the path widened. As the three of them approached, Jake saw an old man sitting in an old rocking chair on the wooden porch. Asleep beside the man was what Jake at first took to be a dog.

They approached the cabin, stopping a few yards from the steps to the porch. The old man said nothing at first, moved not at all as he quietly studied the new arrivals. The animal sleeping beside him shifted, lifted its head and opened its eyes.

Jake realized then that it wasn't a dog, but something like a Little One, a small dragon-like creature similar to what Jake had come across in the Other World of the Dark Castle.

Jake grinned and winked at the Little One. The creature tilted its head and studied Jake. It blinked its eyes several times.

The old man leaned forward in his chair, placed his elbows on his knees and clasped his hands. His words were soft and unhurried.

"Hello, folks."

It was a quiet morning in the Village of the Dragons, as was normal. There was a hint of mist in the air as the dew evaporated and drifted from the surrounding vegetation and across the plaza.

Khol came out of the Grand Hall, having been in an early-morning meeting with Natan. Much of the discussion had been about the ever-increasing disturbances in the web despite the closing of the gates to the Other Worlds. There had also been some speculation as to the fate of Tobias Quigley and the humans' journey along the Dark Path.

Khol was about to step away from the great doors of the Grand Hall when something out in the plaza caught his attention. There was a shimmer of light in the air, the faint fog whorled and was shunted aside. An area eight feet across in the center of the plaza blurred and went out of focus.

A shadow formed in the disturbance, and a moment later Janice stepped out, stepped forward. She frowned darkly and looked about the plaza. Two other humans followed her out of the disturbance and stood behind her.

Janice ignored Khol by design; she stood waiting, almost as if waiting to be welcomed. The portal behind her faded.

Khol walked across the plaza, stopped several paces from the humans.

"Janice," he said, betraying no emotion one way or the other.

Janice glanced briefly at the human-like dragon, said nothing and let her gaze again drift across the village.

"Your presence here is unexpected," said Khol.

"I seek Tobias."

"Tobias is not here."

Janice looked sharply then at Khol. "What has the old man been up to?" she asked.

"I would not know."

Janice looked away dismissively. She silently noted that a number of Jahai, some of them of the heavier species, several others like this humanoid-looking Bentai dragon standing before her, had begun to warily approach.

"I would speak with Natan."

"I'm sure you would. Unfortunately, he is otherwise occupied."

"Advise him of my arrival. I have no doubt that he will want to see me."

"I have no doubt that he is already aware of your presence." Khol stood unmoving.

Janice's expression hardened. "I see. A low-level functionary seeks to rise above his station."

At the human's cold tone, two of the nearer Jahai moved up to stand beside Khol. They took no overt action, but the unspoken statement was made.

The two humans behind Janice responded in kind and moved up to stand beside her. She, however, wasn't about to give this Jahai the satisfaction of intimidating her. She calmly raised a hand, silently indicating that her companions should step back.

She gave Khol a gentle smile.

"It is of little consequence," she said. "I wished only to present myself in audience to your leader upon my arrival in this, his fair community. Please... would you pass along my salutation?"

"As you wish."

"Very well, then." Janice turned from Khol. Her escort moved aside to allow her to pass. She took several steps and slowed. She stopped and looked back.

"The Ancient Guardian..." she said softly, almost but not quite a question.

"What about him?" asked Khol.

Janice smiled thinly. She saw no reason to pursue it further.

"Yes... of course," she said. "I will see you again, Jahai."

She turned from Khol a final time and walked away. Khol watched as Janice raised a hand in front of her and appeared to rest her palm against something he could not see. The air before her shimmered and for just a moment Khol thought he could see something beyond the portal, a small room with furniture or equipment that he did not recognize. It faded as Janice and her companions stepped through.

Khol and the dragons standing beside him were alone in the plaza of the Village of the Dragons.

Tobias placed a foot on the first step, looked up at the old man on the porch.

"Good afternoon to you, sir," he said. "How are you this fine day?"

The old man leaned back, his chair creaking painfully. He scratched at his chin, looked to Jake and Meara, and then back to Tobias.

"I'm doing well enough. I thank you for asking." His tone wasn't overly friendly, but not totally unreceptive either. He was waiting to see where things went. He looked again to the others, again to Tobias. "Yourself?"

"Just fine," said Tobias. "We've been on the trail a spell. Our canteens are getting a bit light. Could you spare some water that we might refill them?"

The old man leaned forward again to the creaking of the chair. He pointed to a hand pump beside the cabin.

"Help yourselves," he stated flatly.

Jake could have sworn the pump hadn't been there before. Meara had the same thought.

"That's downright spooky," she said under her breath, though loud enough for the others to hear.

"I hear that," agreed Jake. He took Meara and Tobias' canteens, went to fill them along with his own. He wanted to be off to one side to better keep an eye on things, to be ready in case things turned unpleasant. He had grown accustomed to things turning unpleasant.

"I don't expect you get much company dropping in," said Tobias.

"You expect right," said the old man. He indicated the Little One beside him. "It's just me and Buddy, most of the time. Kinda prefer it that way, to be honest."

"Oh, I can appreciate that, sir. I surely can." Tobias could hear the water pump screeching as Jake worked the handle. "We'll be on our way just as soon as Jacob over there finishes filling the canteens."

"Don't want you taking offense," said the old man. He settled fully back into this chair. "More comfortable in the quiet, is all."

Meara wondered at the old man's curious choice of words.

"You've been here a long time?" she asked. "On the Dark Path?"

"I don't know from *Dark Path*. Home is home."

Beside the chair, the Little One slowly stood and stretched. It moved up nearer the old man, sat on its haunches and looked directly at Meara. It blinked, cocked its head, straightened. The old man reached out without looking away from the humans, rested a hand on the little dragon. Meara thought she could hear a low, rumbling purr.

"What's his name?" she asked.

"He never told me," the old man said, very matter-of-factly. "I just call him Buddy."

"Sounds about right," Jake grumbled as he returned to the others, handed Tobias and Meara their canteens. He had heard cryptic comments like that in every world he had visited on his quest.

"I thank you for your hospitality, kind sir," said Tobias. He slipped his canteen into its holster. For him, the comment hadn't been cryptic at all. It in fact said a lot. "We'll be on our way."

The old man looked down at the Little One, who appeared to be studying the humans. The dragon rumbled contentedly. "So you shall," he said.

With that, Tobias started away.

Jake took a step to follow, then hesitated and turned back to the old man. "Is there anything we should be watching out for up ahead?"

The old man continued to look down at the Little One. "Wouldn't know. Never been there."

"Right," sighed Jake. "Thanks." He and Meara followed after Tobias.

"He wasn't very informative for a Guardian," mumbled Meara.

"He wasn't the Guardian," said Jake.

Master Peter stood near the short wall enclosing the roof of the Temple's east tower. His hands clasped behind his back, he watched the strange, twisting, spiraling cloud formations in the distance. There was an odd musty smell in the air, drifting in the slight breeze that was brushing across his face. Peculiarly, it reminded him of the old scrolls in the library.

He heard the access door open behind him. Brother John climbed up onto the roof and walked over to stand beside him.

"Brother John." Peter nodded welcome while continuing to look out across the Outland.

"Good afternoon, Master Peter." John studied the sky. "It's not natural," he said.

"No," agreed Peter. "It is not."

Half a minute later, as they watched, the clouds quickly dissipated. The color of the sky returned to a late afternoon steely blue.

"They are more frequent," said John. "Whatever *they* are."

"And more severe," said Peter. "And while I have not noted any destructive effects here, I am reminded that we are not all that there is."

"Yes sir." John looked about the tower roof, out then to the surrounding forests of the Outland. He glanced once and again to Master Peter while never looking directly at him. He looked forward again and quietly cleared his throat.

Master Peter gave the hint of a smile. "What is it, John?" he asked.

"Nothing really," said John. He stumbled through his next words. "Just that we, I... I could not help but notice that you have been spending a lot of time locked away in the library these past days. A lot of time, even for you, sir."

"Have I?"

"Yes." John hesitated. "Master Peter, some have wondered if perhaps your research is related to what has been happening of late... the weather."

Peter turned slightly, let his gaze drift across the treetops of the Outland. Far in the distance, a thinning of the trees showed where the Village of Serpent's Keep was located, less than a day's walk from the temple.

"Brothers will gossip," he said at last. "It is easy to lose oneself when delving into the ancient scrolls."

"Of course, Master. I do not mean to pry." John struggled for a way out. "The ancient language can be quite demanding."

"Translation can be problematic, to be sure." Master Peter turned then to look directly at John. "Have you ever considered the original purpose of our brotherhood, John?"

"We exist but for one purpose, Master Peter. We bear witness to the good and the bad of humankind, that we might answer when called upon."

"Well spoken, Brother John," said Peter. "And just how might we bear that witness, isolated from humankind as we are in this temple?"

"If we are not apart, then we are part, by the very nature of such, and we would lose all objectivity."

"Yes, yes," Peter sighed. "In any event, your response, while well stated, does not actually address the question of the *origin* of our order, or specifically, of the Temple."

"Oh. I see." John was clearly confused. He didn't see. He wasn't completely clear as to the question. "I am sorry. I don't know how to answer."

"Yes," said Master Peter. "No need to apologize, John."

Again the two grew silent, each lost in his own thoughts, each letting his gaze drift out across the Outland. Peter eased out of the silence then, his question spoken softly.

"Have you ever wondered that our order has but one temple?" he asked.

"Such has not occurred to me before now."

They watched then as dark, misshapen clouds began to form once again on the horizon.

"Hmm..." Master Peter sighed.

§

Jake used the side of his foot to push dirt over the small campfire, riling up the glowing coals and sending a puffy plume of smoke into the damp, early morning air. Meara was kneeling a few yards away as she stuffed her few supplies into her small pack.

Their camp was in a grove of apple trees that had long ago gone wild. Tobias was standing a dozen yards from camp, was little more than a shadow near the edge of the grove. Jake came up and stood beside him.

The early dawn sky was quickly brightening. Tobias was looking out across a grassy plain. Jake followed his uncle's gaze. Half a mile away was a silhouette in the predawn light; a solid mass running several miles left to right.

"Is that a wall?" he asked. It was difficult to judge from this distance, but it looked to be twelve to fifteen tall.

"It looks like it," said Tobias absently.

"Was it there before?" Jake had stood at this very spot the night before and hadn't seen anything out there. But it had been dark.

"I expect so. It doesn't matter. It is now." Tobias took a long, deep breath. He was ready to move out. He looked back toward camp. "Let's get our gear."

A warm breeze brushed across the calf-high grass, creating an eerie whispering sound. In the distance, beyond the wall that still lay ahead, the mountain and its castle faded in and out of view as something fog-like drifted before it, between whatever lay ahead and the mountain on the horizon. It was a gray, swirling haze that itself faded in and out, as if one moment real and the next imaginary.

Approaching the wall, they saw that it was constructed of tightly fitted stone, twelve feet high and running left to right as far as they could see.

Directly ahead was a narrow opening in the wall.

"Well, that looks very much like an invite to me," said Tobias, leading the way.

Passing through the opening, they found themselves in a maze of stone walls, each wall tall enough that it made it difficult to use the sky or the world beyond the labyrinth to maintain any sense of direction. Jake insisted that he could do it, so Tobias and Meara quickly allowed him to take the lead.

In a true maze, direction wasn't always your best friend. What Jake tried to focus on was any sort of pattern. This wasn't the first maze that he had come across. There had been the labyrinth below the castle in one Other World and the storm drains beneath the abandoned city in another, just to name two. As a result of his past experiences, he thought himself not bad at navigating such things.

When it came to labyrinths, the whole concept of direction was often used to intentionally mislead. However, you eventually had to get from here to there. Jake understood that much. He also knew that labyrinths were usually designed in patterns, frequently interconnected clusters of mini-labyrinths. He soon found that to be the case with this maze.

Actually, this maze wasn't all that complicated. Jake quickly figured out that the secret to this one was not to overthink it.

It was almost twenty minutes before Jake began hearing faint grumblings from his companions following behind him; a few minutes more and the grumblings began to grow more vocal.

"Master Jacob," Meara started.

"Just up ahead," said Jake, his confidence waning hardly at all. "Not far now."

"Yes sir." Meara silently noted that there was no sign of an exit up ahead. "I'm sorry, sir. I'm not one to doubt, I know that I could do no better, but I can't help but be just a little concerned."

"Not to worry, Meara," said Tobias. "I'm sure Jake will lead us out soon enough."

"Yes sir." She looked back behind them, at the intersection they had just passed. They had just crossed their own footprints.

Rations low, and at best a few days of water.

They might die in here.

Jake noticed then sunlight on the ground ahead, near the next bend. Coming around the corner, it was a straight shot to the opening in the perimeter wall, and clear daylight was streaming in.

He wore a growing smile the others couldn't see, and he breathed out a barely concealed sigh of relief. He stepped through the opening and out of the labyrinth. Several steps out, he sensed that something was wrong, though he didn't know what that wrong was. He slowed, took several more steps. He stopped.

He didn't want to look back.

"Hey guys?" he mumbled. There was no answer. He waited. "Oh, boy."

He had no choice. He looked back over his shoulder.

Yep. There was no one there.

"Oh, geez… not again."

Jake turned fully around.

"Oh, geez," he said again. The opening into the labyrinth was gone. He stepped back to the now solid wall. He pressed a hand flat on the stone, hoping that it was illusion, hoping that the opening was still there. He rubbed his palm against solid stone.

The opening had been a portal, and at the moment that portal was closed.

He turned slowly away from the wall, faced outward then, across an alien landscape. It was a flat plain covered in clusters of low-growing gray vegetation. The sky was a colorless dusk.

The castle was much nearer, its mountainside a purple silhouette sitting high on the near horizon.

§

Tobias and Meara stepped out of the labyrinth, following Jake through the opening. Ahead of them was a flat plain covered in clusters of low-growing gray vegetation. The castle was visible in the distance, set against the mountainside on the horizon, appearing eerily closer.

There was no sign of Jake.

"Sir?" Meara asked anxiously.

"Yes," Tobias stated flatly. "So I see."

Chapter Nine

Mrs. Hodges had spent the afternoon in her back alley booth preparing several orders of her herbal mixtures. There had been an increase in requests for her services of late. It was difficult to ignore the atmospheric disturbances, if they could be called that, and many of Mrs. Hodges' fellow villagers were growing increasingly anxious. Most of the orders were for her calming potions, but there were a surprising number of requests for various first aid mixtures and even a few defensive concoctions as citizens considered the possibility of having to abandon the village for the Outland.

She had to wonder at that, as whatever was happening was obviously not exclusive to the village. What was happening here was happening everywhere.

And really, if it came to that she doubted that many of her friends and neighbors would survive long outside the walls of Serpent's Keep.

Her walk home from the marketplace was quiet; those she passed along the way weren't in the mood for conversation; so much the better. Rounding the corner from the main thoroughfare and looking down the side street, she noticed a figure dressed in heavy monk's robes standing across the road from the estate's main gate, near the entrance to the park.

She stopped at the wrought iron gate of the Quigley Estate and looked across at the monk. She recognized him then.

"Master Peter," she said. "It's been a while."

Peter took that as a sign of welcome and started across the road. They met halfway. "Good afternoon, Mrs. Hodges. Yes, ma'am. It has been several years, at least."

"What brings you to the village?" she asked as they shook hands.

"I was hoping to talk with you."

"With me?" Mrs. Hodges and Peter had a history going back a very long way, but they didn't really know each other very well. Their past relationship was tied to events from long ago and to a handful of shared acquaintances.

"If that is all right with you."

"Of course it is."

It was a pleasant afternoon, and even the intermittent disturbances had eased up some. Mrs. Hodges indicated the park and they walked back to the open gate. The park was empty, as it had been for days as people chose to remain in their homes as much as possible. Mrs. Hodges and Peter worked their way along the winding walkway and settled in at the first table.

She considered starting with small talk, instead got right to it. "What can I do for you, Peter? I assume it has something to do with what's happening..." she pointed a thumb up at the sky.

"In a roundabout way, yes." Peter grew thoughtful. "How to begin..."

Mrs. Hodges waited without comment.

"As you are aware," Peter started again, "our sanctuary is fortunate to have an extensive library, replete with a number of very old volumes."

"I may have heard something to that effect." Of course she had. Though seldom seen by any but the resident monks, the library at the Temple was renowned for its collection of volumes and ancient scrolls.

"Yes, well..." Peter hesitated, continued then, though seeming now to shift direction. "I have recently had cause to reassess the circumstances of our order."

"Oh... I see. The Temple? The brotherhood?"

Peter had spent a significant portion of his life in that musty library. He had spent years hovered over ancient scrolls, deciphering and translating and interpreting the meaning of very cryptic works written in ancient, obscure, sometimes dead languages. But due now to the events of the last few years, he had found reason to revisit many of the most ancient of those scrolls, seen now under the light of a shifting perspective. His translations took on new interpretations.

"Rather surprising, really," Peter wondered aloud. "As inquisitive as I most certainly am by nature, and always have been, the origin of our brotherhood was something that I seldom questioned. I suppose I falsely equated the founding with the purpose, and I let it go at that."

"And now?"

Peter looked directly at Mrs. Hodges. His focus seemed to shift again. "Do you know what Tobias is up to?" he asked.

"I seldom know what Master Tobias is up to," she said matter-of-factly. When she saw that Peter was waiting for more, she went on. "Other than trying to catch up with young Master Jacob, I do not. You can be relatively certain that whatever the two of them are doing, it has something to do with your *roundabout reason* for being here."

"I believe that, and more."

"What do you mean?"

Peter wasn't sure what he meant. He wasn't sure what it was that he knew, nor what he understood of what he knew. He didn't really know how to apply what he believed he knew to the real world.

The real world...

That was almost funny. It wasn't the real world that he was trying to understand. It was rather some bizarre ethereal landscape that Tobias Quigley had travelled for centuries, perhaps millennia, and that Peter had only just become aware.

"There were originally six temples," he said softly. "Six temples, scattered across six worlds, or planes of the same world, whatever that means." He shrugged. "The translation is fuzzy on that; planes of existence, and either different flavors of one world, or similar but different worlds. I'm not sure."

"Ah, you are not sure, but it all reads differently now that you know of the gates."

"And the planes and threads and doors and all that." Another shrug. "Interpretations change, Mrs. Hodges. They evolve. On the one hand it becomes less cryptic, on the other much more confusing."

"I can see how." Mrs. Hodges frowned. "But I don't see how any of that connects with any of what's going on."

"From what I have been able to decipher, I believe that whoever created the gates also created the temples; I just don't know why. I also believe the temples were at one time interconnected, bound... by something."

"You mean physically?"

"I don't know," he said. They had been bound together in some way, but he didn't have any more than that. He suspected that the relationship between the temples had at one time been strong. He was fairly certain that though the temples and the gates had been created by the same entity, they had not been placed on the same worlds.

Except for his own temple and the master gate. Serpent's Gate. That had to mean something. Yet from what he had been able to interpret, his temple had been considered an isolated outpost among the line of temples.

Was there an actual relationship between his temple and Serpent's Gate? If so, was the isolation of his temple from the others tied to that relationship?

The afternoon was growing late, the sky was shading from blue to bright gray. And Peter hadn't gotten any answers. Though, to be fair, he wasn't sure that he had asked an actual question. Certainly not the right question.

He wasn't sure that he knew what that question was.

"What is it you want, Peter?" asked Mrs. Hodges. "Why are you here?"

Peter leaned nearer Mrs. Hodges. She thought she could see a growing desperation in his eyes.

"I don't have it right," he said. "I'm missing something. Our origin. The temples. Something doesn't fit, and it's important. I know it is. I need to talk to Tobias."

"And you think it has something to do with what's happening."

"It may not be related at all. But that is not what troubles me."

"Right. The temples. The six temples."

"Translating the ancient script is imprecise at best. And the original words put to scroll were cryptic to begin with. With my greater awareness of what lay out there, the reinterpretation has left shadows in what I see. There is something incomplete in what I see. I am missing something important."

"You think Master Tobias has the answer?"

"Or he has the question. If he does not, he needs to find it.

Tobias and Meara had been walking for several hours. The world around them was flat and dry, mostly desolate with occasional islands of gray vegetation. The sky overhead was a cloudless, dull, dusky gray. It never changed, never growing darker, nor brighter.

There was no sound, no wind, no movement but for the two humans walking across the barren landscape. The walls of the labyrinth were now far behind them, the silhouette of the mountain range ahead sat low on the near horizon.

They stopped near a small cluster of short shrubs. Meara brought out her canteen and took several long swallows. As Tobias looked curiously around them, an increasing sense of unease weighed on him. He didn't like the feel of this place. It was more alien than any world he had visited, and he had visited a lot of worlds.

He reached out and took hold of a leaf of the nearest bush. It was triangular shaped, pale gray, with thin brown veins. He rubbed it between his fingers. It didn't feel real. None of this felt real.

Meara slipped her canteen back into its belt holster.

"We would have seen him by now, sir," she said. "If he were here."

Tobias let go of the leaf, looked ahead, across the plain in the direction of the mountain and the castle. There was no sign of Jake, but that didn't mean that he wasn't here. He could be here, just not the *same* here.

They had watched him vanish, disappearing before their eyes as he stepped out of the maze ahead of them and onto the plain. This plain. They had followed Jake immediately after exiting the labyrinth, but he was gone.

Tobias was certain that whatever landing Jake had traveled to, he was still on the Dark Path. And if Jake was still on the Dark Path, then the castle would likely be before him, as it was for Tobias and Meara.

"He's here, Meara," he said. He indicated the castle set into the mountainside. "That's where we'll find him."

Traveling back to the Temple after his visit with Mrs. Hodges, Master Peter found himself walking the trail in the dark. He had no interest in spending the night in Serpent's Keep, and he had traveled the Outland at night more than once over the years. The trail running between the village and the Temple was well-traveled and he was quite familiar with it.

Still, even this part of the Outland, between village and temple, could be a dangerous place, all the more so at night. Shadows that kept to the woods during the day crept out onto the trails at night. Peter did his best to keep a watchful eye on his surroundings.

And yet his mind did begin to wander. His conversation with Mrs. Hodges had given him little so far as answers, but it did cause him to reevaluate what information he had brought with him; the origin of the brotherhood and the six temples in which the brotherhood resided; the real purpose of the brotherhood; the cryptic words written on ancient scrolls in all-but-forgotten languages; the library itself.

The night air grew cooler. The animal sounds emanating from the shadows of the forest beyond the trail slowly transformed as creatures of the dark replaced the creatures of the day. A partial moon had already risen and had begun to spread a silvery light across the path in front of him.

Peter did feel ill-at-ease, if only slightly, despite his own self-reassurances, and he grew all the more wary and a bit more watchful.

A strange sensation then; it crept up slowly until it was almost overwhelming. Physical, and yet not. It pulled at him, wore at him, frayed at the edges of his mind. As it spread, he fought to push it away as something unreasonable. But it kept coming back. It stayed with him then. He wasn't sure what it was at first, but it stole into his thoughts and seeded there, the meaning and the imagery growing steadily clearer.

It was as if the world in which he walked wasn't his world at all.

His pace quickened. He would not rest, could not rest, until he was safely within the walls of his temple.

Jake stood with his back to the small campfire. The thick, shoulder-high bushes encircling his campsite shimmered in the firelight, shadows and light dancing among the branches and leaves. Beyond the camp, the vast plain spread out across the landscape in all directions beneath a black night sky filled with sparkling stars.

The silhouette of mountain range on the nearby horizon was a different shade of dark than the sky or plain, and the castle set into the mountainside shone with the glow of the partial moon that was hanging in the sky just above it.

Jake estimated he would reach the castle the following day, this assuming that he got an early start in the morning and there were no unplanned side trips through unexpected portals. He hoped to find Tobias and Meara waiting for him there. He had no doubt that wherever they were, they traveled the Dark Path, and that meant the castle was before them as well.

Jake had been traveling alone for almost two days, ever since stepping out of the labyrinth and starting across the plain. In a strange way it reminded him of his earlier journeys in the Outland and into the Other Worlds. Meara had been his companion on some of those journeys, but he had traveled alone on several of them. He had been hardly more than a boy then, was not much more than that now. And though he could honestly say that he now had a lot more experience, it was equally true that he knew as little about what he was into on this journey as he had known about the portals and the Other Worlds back then.

He stared at the castle in the distance. It seemed almost near enough that he could reach out and touch it. He actually had to hold back lifting a hand.

Tomorrow. Tomorrow he would have answers. He hoped that his uncle and Meara would be there, but with them or alone he would soon stand before the Ancient Guardian.

Chapter Ten

Meara ate the last of her biscuit, washed it down with coffee. She moved away from the fire and stood at the edge of their small camp. Morning was coming, the eastern horizon growing lighter. The mountain range was much nearer, was showing clearer and brighter with the coming dawn. She estimated they should reach the range by nightfall.

Assuming the path from here to there was a straight line, which wasn't something that they could count on.

"Tonight you figure, sir?" she asked.

"Perhaps," said Tobias. He took a last sip from his coffee. He used his foot to push dirt over their dying fire. "Perhaps tomorrow morning."

Meara continued looking to the mountains, to the castle. Was Jake seeing what she was seeing? Was he near the castle? Was he already there?

Her brow wrinkled, a frown forming as a recurring thought pushed to the front of her mind.

What had been the purpose?

She glanced back to Master Quigley, turned again to the mountain range.

"Sir? I don't understand. What good was the quest, Master Jacob gathering the artifacts and closing the gate? He sacrificed so much."

Tobias took a step from the smoking embers, toward Meara. His gaze went past her, out to the plain and beyond, to the horizon.

"It was absolutely critical, Meara. Critical. Closing Serpent's Gate closed the Other Worlds to Janice; closed the worlds of the Jahai to her, as well."

"Pardon, Master Quigley, but isn't she going wherever she wants? Isn't that why we're going to talk to the Ancient Guardian?"

"Oh, not so, my dear." Tobias turned back to the camp and began packing their gear. "The worlds of the gates are quite different from the threads that she is now traveling. The Other Worlds of the gates offered a special access to the planes of the universe; so the Ancient Guardian is said to have designed them. Any worlds or landings that are now accessible across the web of threads are isolated, or are otherwise limited by time or physical presence."

Tobias' last words trailed off. He stared down at his pack, full now and ready to close.

"Sir?" asked Meara.

Tobias had to admit, if only to himself, that he had been surprised at Janice's ability to move from one set of threads to another. She appeared to be creating new threads, or repurposing existing threads, connecting planes and worlds and landings that had up to now been totally distinct from one another.

It didn't look like Janice was yet fully capable of directing her formation of these new threads, but Tobias believed that it was only a matter of time. And until then, she was creating serious disruptions in the fabric of the universe.

Tobias picked up their gear, handed Meara her backpack as he started from camp.

"What say we get this day started," he said.

§

Martin helped Janice step down from the standing frame and guided her over to the stool. Her face was pale, almost gray, her breath feathered and light. This had been a particularly difficult transit, as they usually were when the thread that she repurposed had to support not just her but an escort as well. It didn't matter that the thread was temporary, perhaps even collapsing behind her.

The frustration on Janice's face was visible through her gray countenance. This was her third attempt to reach the Dark Path since her visit to the Village of Dragons. Martin had doubts that Janice, despite her expertise, would be able to reach those planes of the web in which the Dark Path resided.

Janice herself had no such doubts. Her reach had only extended further since escaping the landing in which Tobias Quigley had imprisoned her. She believed that her increasing thread expertise would eventually get her to the Dark Path.

And to Tobias.

Martin handed her a glass of water that was supplemented with a number of nutrients. She took a long drink and gave the glass back.

"Thank you, Martin."

"You can't keep up this pace, Janice." He set the glass on the nearby table. "The next trip or the one after will be one way."

"Don't be so dramatic."

"With each return you are in worse condition than the return before. It's not worth it. He is not worth it."

Janice slid off the stool, using Martin for support. She started toward the door.

"We'll try again tomorrow."

"Janice, please. Two days. At least give it two days."

Janice reached the door. She ignored his pleadings. "I'll be in my room. Wake me for dinner." She held onto the door jamb and looked back over her shoulder. "I need to know what he knows."

She continued into the dimly lit hall without another word, briefly resting a hand on the old wood panel of the opposite wall.

Martin sat on the vacated stool and frowned at the now empty doorway.

Sure, Tobias may have information that Janice wanted, but Martin was certain that she could get by without it. Janice was the scientist, Tobias was not. She knew the web like no one else, excepting perhaps the Ancient Guardian himself.

Martin suspected that Janice may have an underlying fear that Tobias Quigley might again manage to derail the campaign to bring the universe under the blessed umbrella of the Rhetani.

And that Janice would not abide.

Khol's meeting with Natan had gone about as he had expected. Despite recent threats to the web, the leader of the Jahai had in the past repeatedly declined to return to the home world system.

He declined to do so yet again.

The location of the Village of the Dragons had been determined by the location of the hub of threads underlying the site. There were only a few dozen threads in the entire web. Some of those threads, though nowhere near all of them, intersected at several key locations within the web. The Village of the Dragons was one such hub. It tied together a number of important locations of the web, and had been the reason Natan had made this the administrative seat of the Jahai.

But conditions were growing more unstable by the day. Disturbances in the web, having subsided for a time, had returned and were increasing in frequency. The Village of the Dragons was becoming more isolated within the web, and Khol feared that should the situation continue to deteriorate, Natan could be forever cut off from their home system. Threads were not the gates of old, and their routes through the web had been extremely limited to begin with. The more threads that were lost, the more isolated the village became.

Khol stood outside the Grand Hall. There was a small group of dragons standing in the central plaza, all looking up at the sky.

A shattered dome hovered above the world, a spiderweb of thin orange cracks spreading, continuing to slowly spider across the dark gray shell. This continued for another minute as Khol watched. Then, at three points directly overhead, small blue spots formed. These quickly grew, eating at the gray.

An explosion of color then as bright blue suddenly swept across the sky. The gray was abruptly gone, and the world was again as it should be. A single faint wisp of cloud began to form. It drifted as it slowly expanded.

A group of five dragons, all of the sleek, flying Lynhaur species, came out of the Roundhouse, the building that housed the passage stones. They were returning from another journey into the threads. They were exploring each of the threads that emanated from the hub, this their third trip. As they neared, Khol could see that the news was not good.

The village was increasingly cut off from the other landings in the hub, and the hub from the rest of the web. They would soon be all alone.

The five Lynhaur dragons gathered before Khol and the leader of the group stepped out in front of the others.

Khol would be sending them out again, this time into the Dark Path. They must find Tobias and his companions. Tobias must be made aware of recent events.

Chapter Eleven

The front hall felt cool after days of the warm, dry air of the open plain. The room was wide, the ceiling two stories high. A central staircase led from the ground floor up to an abbreviated mezzanine. There were no windows. There were several doors on the main floor, one on the mezzanine.

A handful of narrow tables made of old wood were set along the walls, the only furniture. An old, musty smell emanated from the rough stone walls. There was something very ancient about the room, which was fitting considering the resident of this castle.

Jake walked from the heavy front door into the middle of the front hall. The castle was disconcertingly quiet. He ignored the stairs for now, chose the nearest ground floor door. The hallway that he entered was narrow, the ceiling low, the walls made of the same gray stone as that of the foyer. He passed by a number of open doors, all leading to empty rooms.

Rounding a corner, he saw the shadow of a figure hovering near the next bend. It disappeared beyond the bend as Jake approached. He continued down the hallway and rounded the next corner.

The figure was waiting at a wide archway at the end of the hall, the flickering golden light of a lamp hanging on the wall revealing the man's face; pale skin, dark eyes and heavy brows. He was human, of average height; he wore a heavy brown robe.

Jake stopped midway down the hall. The man's expression didn't change. The dark eyes reflected the light of the lamp as shadows brushed across the face.

The man lifted a hand then, waved for Jake to follow before turning and disappearing around the corner. Jake followed, stepped through the arch and turned down the next hallway; three more steps and he entered a large foyer.

Several hallways emptied into this room. The figure stood before a set of heavy double doors, looking back at Jake, his hands resting on the wooden door handles. As Jake crossed the room and approached, the man pushed down on the handles and pushed the doors inward.

Jake entered a round chamber, forty feet across, with russet-brown stone walls and a domed ceiling. To the left, two high-backed chairs with side tables were set against the wall; a set of French doors just beyond the pair of chairs led outside. Light spilled onto the chamber floor from the doors' inset windows.

Jake was alone, the guide nowhere to be seen. The main feature in the room was what at first looked like a thin curtain of water, four feet across and seven feet tall, that hung midair in the middle of chamber, two feet above the floor. The threshold membrane was half an inch thick, shimmered and sparkled. Jake stood within arm's length of the feature, what he assumed to be a portal. He could see nothing within it, but felt a cool breeze coming from it and pushing against his face.

The French doors opened and a tall, slender man came into the room. He had a thin face, startlingly bright eyes and smile, and long, salt-and-pepper hair. He was wearing loose pants and a long-sleeved shirt, soft shoes.

He was wiping his hands with a cloth hand towel.

"Sorry to have kept you waiting." He almost glided into the room, the doors closing behind him. "I lose track of time when I'm gardening."

"Not a problem," said Jake. There was more than a hint of confusion in his tone.

The Ancient Guardian indicated the portal. "Do you like my magic mirror?"

"Magic mirror?"

"Nah," said the Ancient Guardian, grinning. He stood on the other side of the portal. Jake could just make out the outline of the man. He saw him lift a hand, and a moment later Jake saw a village beyond the threshold. Figures were moving about in the central plaza. Dragons.

"A window," said the Ancient Guardian. Another wave of a hand. The image changed. It was another village, this one on an open plain, the sun high in the sky.

Another wave of the hand and the portal membrane again took on the illusion of a thin, watery curtain. The Ancient Guardian stepped around the feature and moved up beside Jake. He indicated the nearby chairs and started toward them, again wiping his hands with the small towel.

"It is good to finally meet you, Jacob Quigley," he said.

This really wasn't what Jake had expected. He nonetheless tried to keep the growing doubt out of his voice. "Are you the Ancient Guardian?"

The Ancient Guardian smiled as he tossed the towel onto a side table.

"Call me Aldwyn. Please."

"Aldwyn."

"Thank you."

Jake's guide reappeared, coming in through a narrow door a third of the way around the circular chamber. He was carrying a silver tray with a teapot and two cups.

"Thank you, Corwin," said Aldwyn.

Corwin set the tray onto one of the tables, turned half about and gave a slight nod. He picked up the hand towel and left the room as quickly and quietly as he had arrived.

Aldwyn poured tea, indicated one empty chair as he sat down in the other.

"Friend Jacob Quigley. What have you been up to?"

The edge of the plain pushed up against the rolling hills that quickly gave way to the steep side of the mountain. The castle was set into the mountainside, appearing as if it had always been there. It was as dark and ominous as the surrounding landscape, its smooth surface shimmering in the fading light of the setting sun.

It was obvious to both Tobias and Meara that they wouldn't be able reach it before nightfall, and decided to spend a night in the lower hills and make their way into the mountains and then on to the castle in the morning.

For Meara, it was maddening to have to stop for the night when they were so close. It had been an uneventful trek across the plain and they had made good time. The nearest hills were no more than half an hour away. But they were both exhausted, and they didn't feel it would be safe to head into the mountains in the twilight.

Something made Tobias slow his pace, his footfalls easing, his steps shortening. Something was brushing at his mind, leaving a faint imprint that slowly faded.

He stopped then. Meara came to a stop beside him. She gave him a questioning look.

He turned about, looked back along the path they had been traveling. There was nothing; only the open plain as far as the eye could see.

And then... a rippling in the air, a disturbance some hundred feet or more back along their path. Something was forming, coalescing, hovering just above the ground, several feet across.

"A portal," said Meara.

Tobias said nothing, took a step toward the portal, a second step. He stopped.

Janice... he thought to himself.

The portal struggled to come into existence. Tobias felt its presence, a hot prickly sensation on his skin, on his mind. There was a smell in the air, like electricity running along too-thin wiring.

Tobias took several more steps toward the disturbance. Meara followed cautiously beside him.

The portal began to fade, the rippling in the air to smooth.

Gone then, Janice appeared in place of the portal; she was down on one knee, the fingertips of one hand resting on the surface of the hard ground. She slowly lifted her head as Tobias approached. Her skin was pale, waxy, her eyes set deep in gray.

"You don't look at all well, my dear," he said, managing to sound casual. Meara stood beside him, looking down on the kneeling stranger.

"I've been better," said Janice. She rose deliberately to her feet. Only then did she realize she had come through alone. She hoped her two escort were safely back at the lab and that they hadn't gotten lost in the thread.

She struggled to keep her thoughts from showing on her face. She looked over at Meara, then back to Tobias. There was no sign of Tobias' nephew, Jacob Quigley.

"D'you lose the kid?" she asked.

"He lost us." His brief smile faded. "Is your presence here by chance or intended?"

"I have been looking for you."

"Is that so?" Tobias took a short step closer to Janice; she took a stumbling half step backward; he retreated back a step. "Your efforts are clearly coming at great cost, Janice. To what end?"

"No cost is too great in the service of the cause."

"The glorious Rhetani resolution? To spread acquiescent sunshine across all the universes?"

"Do not mock, Tobias."

"What do you want, Janice?"

She visibly ceded then. "I need your help."

Well, that is certainly unexpected...

"That you would need my help I find unlikely. That you would seek out my help in any event I find most unlikely indeed."

"And yet here I stand before you."

"Yes. Most curious," said Tobias. He paused a moment. "And just what form might this help take?"

"A map."

"A map?"

"The web. The primary landings. The secondary threads."

"You expect me to help you build a new gateway system?"

"I will get there. You have to know that I will get there."

"Will you? Look at the disruptions that you're causing, Janice. You're tearing the web apart, the very fabric of the universe."

Janice was growing noticeably weaker, her face increasingly gray.

"It doesn't have to be so, Tobias," she said tiredly. "With a map..."

"I have no map. Had I such a map, you have to know that I would never help you."

"No one was as close to Aldwyn as you," said Janice. "Other than Aldwyn, no one was as involved in the gateways."

"The gateways were but a small component of the web, Janice. You more than anyone—"

"I know the science. You know the design."

"I do not. Is this what brought you here?"

"We were friends once, Tobias. You, me, Marcus, Nehman, all of us." She nodded toward the castle. "Even Aldwyn. Comrades all, bound by honor."

"Bindings pulled apart by fanaticism and a twisted sense of what it means to be honorable."

"That is unfair, Tobias. The path of the Rhetani is noble and just."

"It is cultish religious extremism and so far beneath you, Janice."

Came the sound then of a number of leathery wings beating at the air. Meara saw shadows drift across the ground about them, skim over Tobias and the strange woman. She looked up, saw the silhouettes of five flying dragons set against the evening sky, circling overhead.

"More company," she said.

Thunder of dragons, Tobias thought to himself. *Traveling the Dark Path?*

"An unexpected turn of events," he said. "The second in an hour."

Meara brought her gaze back to Janice.

"Chance or related?"

Janice's response was to Tobias. "I suspect their purpose is as mine."

"To see us."

"The eminent Tobias Quigley." She took a step back, and another. She kept a close eye on the young woman who was standing next to Tobias. She had the uneasy feeling that if given the chance, the woman would attack, would try to stop her from leaving.

Meara meanwhile watched with a cool, steady gaze. Janice raised a hand, holding up two fingers. Behind her, a portal began to form. The effort shown on Janice's face, draining color, draining what energy she had left to her. She took another step back, moving nearer the still-forming portal.

Meara stood unmoving beside Tobias; he nonetheless reached out and took her arm.

Janice looked at Tobias.

"This cannot end here, Tobias. Your refusal to see the truth will lead only to ill." She stepped back the rest of the way into the portal. The portal quickly dissolved, taking Janice with it.

With Janice gone and the portal closed, the dragons overhead circled a final time and then descended to the ground. They formed a circle around Tobias and Meara.

The leader stepped forward.

"Tobias Quigley," he stated firmly. To Meara then, "Companion."

"Meara," she grumbled.

"Yes."

"Your presence is most unexpected, friend," said Tobias.

"We enter Dark Path. We travel Dark Path. We find you."

"And so you have," said Tobias. "It must be important."

"Khol want Tobias Quigley know, Village of Dragons alone soon."

Tobias considered the meaning of the statement. "The threads?" he asked.

"Threads go."

"I see," said Tobias. He turned to Meara. "Time is not our friend."

"We must get to the Ancient Guardian," said Meara. "We must find Master Jacob."

Tobias turned again to the dragon. "Thank you, friend. You may return to the Village, your mission complete."

"We watch."

"We'll be fine, friend. Thank you."

"We watch."

Tobias considered, nodded agreement.

"Of course. You watch." He looked to Meara. "A walk in the dark after all, my dear."

It was early afternoon in the village of Serpent's Keep, and the day was pleasant. There were only a few wispy clouds in the blue sky and the midday sun was bright and its rays warm. Mrs. Hodges was sitting at a bench in the park opposite Quigley Estate, just finishing a light lunch. There were a number of others in the park, some sitting at picnic tables, others lounging out on the lawn, all enjoying the day.

The world had calmed down of late. There hadn't been a disturbance in several days and people were again daring to come out of their homes and into the daylight.

With lunch over, Mrs. Hodges decided to take a walk before returning to the mansion. She left the bench, followed the walkway around the park, taking a moment now and then to stop and say hello to folks that she passed. She eventually left the plaza through the entrance that opened out onto the main thoroughfare.

The village main gate was to her left. The double-gate was open and even at this distance she could see Mason standing just beyond. His back was to the gate, his attention on something outside the village.

She considered leaving him to his solitude, but her own curiosity got the best of her. He was obviously drawn to something out there and with all that had been happening, and it might be something that she would want to know about.

Walking through the open gate, she acknowledged the one guard standing watch and stepped up beside Mason. Ahead of them, a dusty dirt road wound its way across a sparse landscape of scrub oak, thorny brush and dry grass. She didn't see anything to warrant Mason's focus. He was just staring at the emptiness that was spread out to the south of the village.

"Good afternoon, Mason," she said.

"Ma'am." Mason said without turning to look at Mrs. Hodges.

Mrs. Hodges looked thoughtfully at the narrow road leading away from the village. She had never traveled that road. She had lived in Serpent's Keep her entire life, and other than a handful of trips to the farm to the north she had seldom left the village. She knew that to be true for most of the citizens.

"I sometimes forget how isolated we are," she said.

"Ma'am," Mason said again, distantly.

Mrs. Hodges looked back over her shoulder, back into the village. Okay then... she might as well get back to work. "Well..." she started.

"Our isolation may be greater than you know," said Mason.

"Oh, I don't know about that, Mason. I'm thinking we're pretty isolated."

Mason turned to her for the first time. "There hasn't been a bus arrived from the outside in months."

"Is that really so unusual? Visits from the outside have always been rare."

"The last bus to come to the village was the one that brought Jacob Quigley."

That startled Mrs. Hodges. How could that be so? Jacob had returned to Serpent's Keep not long after Tobias' disappearance. It had been the reason for Jacob coming home. It had been the start of his quest for the artifacts, his travels into the Other Worlds.

Several years ago, at least.

"That... is curious," she said.

"This is not right, Mrs. Hodges. This is most definitely not right."

Where are you going with this, Mason?

"Mason," she started cautiously. "What are you trying to say?"

Mason indicated the open landscape before them. "I don't think the outside is out there anymore."

It was a bizarre suggestion, and very much something that Mason would say. At the same time, if anyone but Mason had said it, Mrs. Hodges would have immediately dismissed it as crazy. But Mason saw things no one else saw. He didn't always see things as they were, but there was usually something there.

Mrs. Hodges felt a numbness spreading throughout her body. She felt cold and hot at the same time.

"Mason?" she prompted.

Mason turned and looked at her, yet wasn't looking at her. There was something distant in his gaze. He turned again to the world out there, to the world that wasn't there.

Mrs. Hodges looked again at the dusty road that wound through the landscape south of Serpent's Keep.

Where did it go? What was out there?

"I should probably get back," she said. "A lot of work to do..."

Mason said nothing. Mrs. Hodges backed away from him, turned about and walked past the man standing watch at the gate, continued into the village. She walked through the park on her way back to the estate. It was even busier than before, as more couples and more families came out of their homes to picnic in the afternoon sun.

Despite the sights and sounds of villagers out enjoying the day, Mrs. Hodges felt very alone. She returned warm greetings and smiling faces with barely an acknowledgment. She reached the park's north entrance and stepped out onto the side street, the Quigley Estate across the narrow road.

Mr. Griffin was standing on the front porch, his hands clasped in front of him, his focus up and past Mrs. Hodges.

She opened the wrought-iron gate and walked up to the front steps.

"Good afternoon, Mr. Griffin." She climbed the steps and stood beside him. She turned and tried to follow his gaze. There was nothing to see.

"Mrs. Hodges," he said softly. There was nothing more.

"I had an odd conversation with Mason a bit ago," she said at last, mostly to fill the quiet space, and perhaps to push unsettling thoughts out into the open.

"Did you?" He didn't sound all that interested.

"I did," she said. "Most odd."

"Yes..." Mr. Griffin said absently. "To be expected, I suppose."

Okay. He had a point. It was Mason, after all.

"I guess so," she said, but doubted that she would be able to let it go. This had been different. Beyond odd, this had struck a nerve. She had sensed real truth in Mason's vision. Yes, it could still mean just about anything, and yet Mason's words had managed to draw her in.

I don't think the outside is out there anymore...

Mrs. Hodges looked side-glance at the stalwart figure standing beside her; a silent presence, preoccupied. *What is he doing out here?*

Mr. Griffin seemed to read her thoughts.

"The mansion is acutely quiet of late, Mrs. Hodges."

How curious. She and Mr. Griffin often spent weeks looking after an otherwise empty estate. Such was the way with Master Tobias, and later with young Jacob.

"They will be home soon," she said.

Mr. Griffin pushed his chin out, drew it back in. "I sense..." he started, then took a long, deep breath. "I am uncertain."

"I am not," Mrs. Hodges said decisively. "They will be home soon. Meara has chores."

Chapter Twelve

After a brief walk in the garden, Jake and Aldwyn returned to the chamber through the French doors. The conversation to now had been light, drifting from one unrelated topic to another with no real direction. Aldwyn had done most of the talking, clearly enjoying having someone new to talk to.

The subject returned to Janice as they circled the window portal in the center of the chamber. The issue of Janice had come up several times during their stroll in the enclosed garden.

"Serpent's Gate and its associated gateways cannot be reopened," said Aldwyn. "Janice knows this. She instead seeks to overlay the sealed passageways with a gate system of her own. With a new system in place, she would open all the universes to the Rhetani."

The Rhetani; a cultish society from Earth's own future. Given the opportunity, their control would spread from their home world and their time to all worlds and all times... to all universes.

Janice was intent on creating that opportunity.

"Can she actually do it?" asked Jake. "Can she make a new gateway system?" From what Jake understood, Janice's abilities, as extensive as they at first appeared to be, were limited. He was given to believe that while she was creating portals, they were limited in scope, time and worlds, and were often temporary. A gateway system to replace Serpent's Gate would cross universal planes and time, would span the entire web of the universe.

"She is quite resourceful, and her abilities are evolving," said Aldwyn "But understand, she is not actually creating new threads. The web has all the threads that it will ever have. Janice is acquiring existing threads and is attempting to repurpose them in order to construct a gateway system."

"That is possible?"

"I do not think so. And almost certainly not one of the scope that Janice is attempting."

"But she thinks she can."

"She is obsessed by her purpose. Such is the failing of the zealot." Aldwyn stood before the portal. "I believe the greater danger, by far the greater danger, is the disruption that is created by her efforts. She is tearing apart the web of the universe. Worlds are being thrown into chaos, landscapes laid waste; entire planes are being set adrift."

Entire planes set adrift...

"Can't you stop her?"

"I cannot. I am forever bound to this place." Aldwyn held a hand out to the window portal, palm out as if resting it against the thin veil between planes. "My vision is far, my reach limited." He turned then to look at Jake. "But you can, Jacob Quigley. And that is why you are here. Is it not?"

Despite their concerns about traveling rough, uneven and unfamiliar terrain at night, Tobias and Meara set out in the early evening and traveled until it was too dark to see. They rested then for several hours, ate from their rations, and set out again when the half-moon rose and spread silvery light across the world. The rolling hills had hours earlier given way to steeper terrain, and with the moon glow they were able to follow the seldom-used trail that wound its way up to the castle.

They approached the castle several hours before sunrise, the half-moon already sinking to the horizon. The night air was cool, and there was a bit of a breeze. High above them, they could just make out the silhouettes of the dragons circling overhead. As they watched, the dragons turned back one by one, heading back along the way of the Dark Path.

Tobias and Meara took the stone steps up to the heavy front door, made of dark wood, black metal bands and large hinges. The door opened as they took the last step.

A middle-aged man wearing a heavy brown robe waited for them in the center of the front hall. He nodded welcome as the door closed behind them.

"Master Quigley," he said calmly. "It has been a long time."

"That it has, Corwin." Tobias gave a warm smile. It held the hint of nostalgia. "A distant time in a faraway land."

He indicated Meara. "This is my traveling companion, Miss Meara Gyles."

"Miss Gyles." Corwin nodded a second welcome, then looked again to Tobias before turning toward one of the hallways. "This way, please."

They followed him down one hall, then another. Meara wanted to ask Tobias how he had come to know this man in a castle at the end of the Dark Path, but each time she started to speak up, their guide looked back to urge them on as he rounded one corner and then another corner.

They came into a small foyer. Across the room was a set of double doors. Passing through, they entered a round chamber with a domed ceiling. The main feature was what looked like a portal hanging above the floor in the middle of the room. Jake and the Ancient Guardian were sitting in a pair of chairs near French doors.

Corwin silently dismissed himself with a curt nod of the head, leaving Tobias and Meara to cross the room on their own. Jake and Aldwyn stood at their approach.

"Friend Tobias," said Aldwyn. He smiled at Meara. "And this must be Meara. I trust your journey wasn't too difficult."

"Not too bad," said Meara.

"Good, good." Aldwyn turned back to Tobias. "Tobias, we weren't expecting you until later this morning."

Tobias told of their exchange with Janice, then of the arrival of the Jahai, of their fears regarding the disruptions in the web. With that, Tobias and Meara had decided to travel the night, to reach the castle as soon as possible.

Aldwyn took the news without comment, then walked the several steps toward the window portal. Tobias followed along beside him, leaving Jake and Meara to wait by the chairs. Aldwyn told Tobias that he had been witnessing the disruptions and shared the concern of the Jahai.

Watching Tobias and Aldwyn in quiet conversation near the portal, Jake saw two old friends getting together after a long time apart. Meara saw it, too.

"I think they were closer than Master Tobias has let on," she said.

"Aldwyn told me they were as brothers," said Jake. He shrugged. "We talked. We've been up all night anticipating your arrival."

"So you knew we were coming..."

"Aldwyn sees much."

"I must say, he is not what I was expecting," said Meara.

He hadn't been what Jake had been expecting, either. But after spending a day and a night with Aldwyn, the Ancient Guardian could have been no one other than Aldwyn.

"Aldwyn was the first human to meet the Jahai," said Jake. He sounded rather retrospect. "They accepted him as one of their own; he lived among them for a time. He told me that he admired their integrity and their moral character. It was he who founded the Guardians when Tobias separated Serpent's Gate and scattered the artifacts across the Other Worlds."

"He really is ancient."

Jake looked about the chamber. "The castle is a place out of time," he said. "And so, therefore is he."

They watched Aldwyn turn from the portal and place a hand on Tobias' shoulder. The Ancient Guardian smiled warmly and said a few more words, then the two of them walked back to Jake and Meara.

"I so wish we had more time, my friend," said Aldwyn, speaking to Tobias while looking at the entire group. "But as has been stated, time is short."

Tobias agreed. "Perhaps when our task is completed, time for a true visit, you and I."

"Perhaps," said Aldwyn, but there was little behind the word. He looked to Jake. "Jacob knows the path you must take. His spirit is strong, and I am certain all will be well in the end."

They stood at the top step, the castle's large front door quietly closing behind them. The sky was brightening, with dawn now only minutes away. The air was still cool.

"He told you what we had to do; right, sir?" asked Meara.

"That he did," said Jake. "Apparently, it is possible to isolate a part of the web from the rest of the web. So he says. Once we do that, Janice will be trapped there, the rest of the web safe."

"Pardon, sir. Didn't Master Quigley trap Janice once before?"

Tobias held his face to the first rays of the rising sun. "The landing on which she had been confined yet remained a part of the web," he said. *It should have held her forever. I underestimated her abilities…*

"I'm supposed to cut away part of the web," said Jake. "Whatever trouble Janice manages to stir up will be kept there."

"Right, sir," said Janice. "And how do we do that?"

"Simple. I travel a thread and close it at the other end. That should separate a small section of the web."

"And that's where she is?"

"So I'm told."

"Pardon again, Master Jacob, but isn't that what you did last time?"

"I would argue that it wasn't a thread the last time, but yeah, pretty much the same."

Tobias shook his head. "The closing of the gates prevented the Rhetani from accomplishing their goal."

"And so Janice is trying to create a new system," said Jake. "Aldwyn doesn't think she can, but her attempt is trashing the fabric of the universe."

"Yes sir," said Meara.

The thread that Jake needed to close was one of the handful of threads that made up the hub underlying the Village of the Dragons. It was the only thread that connected a small segment to the rest of the web. It had to be closed at the far end in order to permanently sever that segment. If the thread was closed at the hub, the thread would remain a part of the isolated section and could theoretically be reattached to the web somewhere else.

"Okay, so you travel the thread, close it on the other side," Meara stated.

"Right."

"While you're on the other side."

"Right."

"Just like last time."

"Pretty much."

"Except, it sounds like there won't be any coming back this time."

"It looks that way."

For Tobias, there was something more, something about that isolated location in the web. It would be more involved than what Jake had been led to believe.

Typical Aldwyn.

"I'll take care of this, Jake," he said. "When we get back to the village, you and Meara head on to Serpent's Keep."

"No sir," said Jake. "Aldwyn was clear. This one is on me."

Tobias glowered for several moments, his eyes focused on the sunrise.

"Very well," he stated at last. "But you won't be going alone."

Chapter Thirteen

Khol walked across the central plaza toward the Grand Hall. The sky overhead was pale lavender, the shadows in the surrounding forest beyond the buildings of the village were tinted a grayish purple.

There were very few Jahai about. Their changing world was making them increasingly anxious and most would just as soon stay under shelter.

He entered the building, walked across the front hall and passed through the open double doors into the audience chamber of the Grand Hall.

Natan was seated on his throne, talking with a small group of Bentai Jahai who were standing at the foot of the platform. Khol stepped to one side in the hall and waited. Several of the larger Thrauhm dragons were slumbering along the wall.

The conversation ended and the group of Bentai started down the center of the chamber. One gave Khol a long, slow half-bow as they passed. They closed the double-doors as they left.

Khol approached the throne. Natan stood and stepped off the platform as Khol neared.

"What news, my friend?" he asked.

"Such news as we have is more grim this day than the last, more grim still than the day before."

"The threads?" Natan began pacing thoughtfully back and forth in front of the platform.

"Another is lost to us," said Khol. "Those that remain do not always lead to where you expect."

Natan briefly looked side-glance at Khol in silent response.

"Natan..." Khol steeled himself for his next statement. "Again, we should consider the journey home. I fear the path may already be lost to us."

The way home had always been a series of primary threads and side passages. The route was now all the more circuitous without the main passages.

Natan stopped his pacing. He stared out across the hall, though what he was looking at was worlds away.

He slowly turned then and looked broodingly at Khol. He gave a grumbling sigh and shook his head as he took the steps up the platform.

"No, my friend." He rested a clawed hand on the arm of the throne. "Whatever our isolation here may be, it is nothing as that of the home worlds. If we are to continue to serve, in whatever limited capacity may remain to us, we must stay here."

Khol hesitated, then acknowledged with a respectful nod. "Yes, Natan."

Natan shifted about and sat again on his heavy wooden throne.

"To those of our brethren whom you are able to reach, call them to us," he stated. Natan didn't like the thought of Jahai being forever stranded alone in far off lands should the frayed web be forever pulled apart. They had lost enough with the closing of the gates. To lose these few side passages as well would remove all hope of those in outlying lands to return here to the Village of the Dragons, worse yet to return to the home worlds.

"Yes, Natan." Khol straightened, turned about and started away from the throne.

"Khol," Natan called after him.

Khol stopped and turned about. "Sir?"

"Tobias Quigley."

"I shall escort him here immediately upon his return."

Natan nodded, leaned back in his chair. Khol waited.

"Friend Khol," Natan stated at last. "We shall get through this."

"Yes, Natan." Khol accepted the dismissal, turned about again and left the hall.

Brother John opened the door to the library and quietly entered the room. The walls were lined floor to ceiling with shelves of old volumes; midway down the room an entire section of the wall was covered with a honeycomb of diamond-shaped compartments stuffed with scroll tubes.

Master Peter was sitting at one of the tables in the middle of the room, his back to John. A lone lamp illuminated an unrolled scroll that was spread out across the table before him.

John walked around the table and stood facing Peter. He waited in silence. It was some time before Peter sensed a presence in the room. He looked up from the ancient scroll.

"Yes, John?" he asked blearily.

"Master Peter," John said softly. "My apologies."

Peter struggled to come out of the misty world that he had been wandering around in; how long, he had no idea. He stretched and leaned back in his chair.

"Not at all, John. What is it?"

"If you have a few moments, sir, I would like to show you something."

"Of course," said Peter. When after a few moments John had yet to show him anything, Peter grasped that he was meant to follow John to whatever it was that he intended to show him. He slid his chair back and stood up. "Lead on then, Brother."

They left the library and started down the hall toward the front of the temple. There was no one about. The halls, rooms and cells all were dark but for an occasional night lamp glowing low. Peter hadn't realized that it was so late. He had been in the library all evening and likely half the night.

They reached the foyer and John quickly stepped ahead and opened the front door. The night air that pushed into the room was cool and refreshing. Peter stepped outside, John right beside him. They moved out onto the porch and stood at the top step. Ahead of them, the open space in front of the temple was dark, empty. The forest beyond the clearing was pitch black.

Peter was about to ask what it was that he was meant to see when he chanced to glance up at the night sky.

Something wasn't right.

The stars had lost their sparkle. They looked... smeared. And they all had an odd color to them; almost lavender.

"Well, that is certainly peculiar," said Peter.

"Do you see it, sir?" ask John.

Peter suspected that he was meant to see more than smeary stars. "See what, John?"

John gave a nod to the sky. "There, Master Peter; between us and the rest of the universe."

"I'm sorry, John. I don't see—" Peter started, then stopped.

Yes. He did see something. There was a film, a shell... something. There was indeed something up there, hovering up there, somewhere between the temple and the stars.

"What is that?" he asked, not expecting an answer.

"A bubble," said John. "We're inside a bubble. The temple, the Outland... we are inside. The rest of the universe... is outside."

Peter took a few moments to study the strange occurrence. The filmy bubble wasn't completely transparent, which was why the stars appeared smeary and off-color. He couldn't tell how much of the world it enclosed, but looking closely, he did see a very gradual curve to the shell. The tall trees encircling the temple prevented any real examination of the sky near the horizon.

Brother John interrupted his thoughts. "Master Peter? What should we do?"

"What do you suggest, John?"

As he asked the question, Peter saw John's face suddenly take on a glow, which quickly spread to the entire porch, the clearing and the forest. Looking again to the sky, Peter saw that the shell had grown opaque, was shimmering a bright, very pale violet hue now shadowing the world.

It faded then, slowly, leaving behind the filmy shell, which itself then slowly dissipated. The stars returned, sparkling against a clear black night sky.

To all appearances, all was as it had been.

"I'm off to bed, then," said Peter. He managed to sound a lot more perky than he felt. "It'll be morning before you know it. Eh, John?"

JohPa was of the Bentai Jahai. He was young, still had quite a bit of growing to do; at least another few inches. Even for a Bentai, his facial features were less reptilian, more humanoid than many of his brethren. His eyes were set closer together, his snout was almost petite.

He stood just off-trail near the gated entrance to the Dark Path. He absently scratched at an itch at the back of his head, sighed a noisy, bored sigh. He had been standing there for two hours, and had another hour before he was due to be relieved.

The world around him, the world around the entirety of the Village of the Dragons, was bathed in an unsettling gray with a tint of some color that he didn't recognize. He had never seen such a color. There was no such color.

He glanced up at the shell of sky. Yes. It was most unsettling.

He scratched again at the itch.

A sound came from the gate; wood striking wood, three times. JohPa stepped onto the trail and to the gate. He lifted the wooden crossbar and moved aside. The gate opened and the humans came through.

"Thank you, friend," said Tobias.

"Welcome, friend Tobias Quigley, and companions," said JohPa. He watched as one of the companions closed the gate. He then replaced the crossbar before stepping past them and led the way back along the trail into the village. Along the way he heard the humans commenting to one another about the changes to the sky, the odd color... and the ominous silence.

Yes, thought JohPa. *Unsettling.*

Khol was standing in the village center, as if he had been expecting Tobias' return.

"Welcome, friend Tobias," he said. He spoke then to the entire group. "I am pleased that you return safely."

"Thank you, friend Khol," said Tobias. He looked curiously about the village, at the sky above that seemed to be pushing down on them. "We are pleased to be back."

"The answers you sought?"

"Our journey was successful."

"Again, I am pleased." Khol looked to the young Jahai. "JohPa, escort our friend Tobias to Natan."

JohPa gave a curt bow of the head in response and started in the direction of the Grand Hall, leaving Tobias to follow after him. At the same time, Khol indicated that Jake and Meara should follow him in another direction, to the human quarter of the village.

They looked from Tobias to Khol.

"Okay, then," said Jake. He and Meara fell in step behind Khol and they started across the plaza. "Is everything all right here, Khol?"

"Everything not all right, Jacob Quigley," said Khol.

Chapter Fourteen

Martin poured another cup of coffee and leaned back against the counter. He took a sip, looking over the rim of the cup at his small lab: a well-organized mess; a cluster of tiny, well-lit islands of work tables in a sea of subdued lighting and shadow.

His life was slowly being eaten away, here, in this room; twelve to fourteen hours a day, seven days a week, week after week, month after month.

He wanted to go home.

Martin had joined Janice and the others on their divine mission to bring all into the way of the Rhetani; all worlds, all times, all universes, all to be embraced by the guiding hand of the Rhetani.

Unfortunately, those who would challenge the cause had managed to shut down the gates. Martin found himself alone, isolated on a world and in a time not his own. For how long, he did not know; perhaps for years. And then Janice, escaping a prison of her own, had found him and brought him here.

Again he served the cause. Now, however, it was sometimes difficult for Martin to draw the line between their actions and the purpose. What he was doing was necessary if Janice was to again reach out, to connect, and to bring all into the way; and yet...

Week after week, month after month...

A figure stood in the doorway; a silhouette, backlit by the light from the hallway beyond. Janice came into the room, worked her way through the work tables to the standing frame set against the back wall. She rested a hand on one of the frame's arm supports.

"You grow weary of this, Martin," she said, without looking at him. "I understand."

"I admit that I long to go home, ma'am."

"And yet there is the purpose."

"Yes, ma'am."

Janice turned then to look at Martin. She wore a slight smile.

"You are faithful, Martin. You would not abandon the cause, nor me."

"I would not."

Janice looked side-glance at the standing frame, her hand still resting upon it.

"I too miss home," she sighed "I sometimes fear that the cause, the mission, will forever keep us from returning. If that be so, it is the sacrifice we must accept."

"It has been such a long time, Janice. Can we be certain the wants of the council are unchanged?"

Janice's expression grew hard. "The Way does not change."

"Of course not. But the means by which we might serve the needs of the Way may have."

Janice stepped away from the standing frame, slowly moved across to the nearest table. She was still very weak from the most recent series of passages through redirected threads. Standing now in the half-shadow between work stations, her sallow face was all the more striking. She used the table for support.

"Our path has been set for us, Martin," she said. "There are no alternative paths for us. We have no choice but to follow what has been given us. Our journey home, should we one day be so fortunate, lay on the same path as the purpose. We cannot reach the one without the other."

Martin held tightly to his cup. The coffee was already turning cold.

"Yes, ma'am," he said haltingly. He knew that however Janice's observation might be true, so too was what that meant should they fail. The very actions they were taking could very well forever close that path to them. The Way, and home, might both be lost to them.

The very fabric of the universe may well be coming apart as key threads were pulled free; threads that Janice had pulled free in order to repurpose. Events were now taking shape on their own, acting on their own, beyond Janice's control, beyond Janice's vision.

What might be happening out there of which they knew nothing?

Janice continued to use the table for support, looked back across at the standing frame. "You have input the data?"

Martin set his coffee cup on the counter behind him. "I have."

"Good." Janice pursed her lips, sighed. "Perhaps..."

"Ma'am?"

Janice frowned, pushed away from the table. She turned to the door. "Tomorrow, Martin. Tomorrow is fine."

"Yes, ma'am. All will be ready."

Jake circled the small campfire and sat on one of the three wooden stools. He picked up the long stick on the ground beside him and used it to poke at the coals glowing at the base of the flames.

Dusk had come, and the strangely tinted gray that enveloped the dragons' village was growing darker. The flickering light of the fire was reflected in the encroaching dark mist.

Jake glanced up at a figure approaching from the direction of the village, looked back then to the fire and waited. Meara came into the light of the fire and sat on the stool beside Jake. She had taken a walk after their evening meal, had been gone for quite a while.

"It sure is quiet," she said. "Eerie."

"They're spooked," said Jake. Dragons liked the dusk. It was their favorite time of day. With the recent sunset, the village should be bustling with activity, both on the ground and overhead. Yet there was hardly a dragon to be seen.

"Them and me both, sir," said Meara. The words faded into the surrounding quiet. They both drifted into their own thoughts, mesmerized by the flickering orange and red of the fire, the pulsating glow of the underlying coal.

They were startled back to the real world when Tobias was suddenly standing before them on the other side of the campfire.

"Uncle Tobias," said Jake. "You missed dinner."

"I can fix you something, sir," said Meara.

"No, no. Quite all right, my dear." Tobias took a seat on the last of the three stools. "I may have a bite later."

They waited for Tobias to say something more, to tell them of his meeting with Natan. He said nothing, quietly stared into the fire.

"Tobias?" Jake prompted finally. "How'd it go? You were gone a long time."

"Yes," said Tobias. "There was much to discuss. Natan is quite concerned."

"We gathered as much," said Jake. "We managed to get a few words out of Khol."

"Of course." Tobias nodded thoughtfully.

"Things are getting worse, aren't they, sir?" asked Meara. "Khol mentioned the threads. He said that Natan is calling everyone home."

"True, true," said Tobias. "A most difficult task, I'm afraid. What with the issue with the threads, reaching their brethren is proving problematic."

"Is there anything we can do?" asked Meara.

"We keep going," Jake stated.

"Exactly so," said Tobias. "We push on. A night's rest, and we continue on in the morning. Which means we'll need to be up well before dawn." Tobias looked up from the fire, out to the night that was quickly coming. He could see nothing; it would take time for his eyes to adjust after the light of the campfire. "It is quiet this evening."

"That it is," said Jake.

When Meara came out of the hut early the next morning, Tobias and Jake were already up. Tobias was putting a few final items into his backpack, while Jake was eating from a block of cheese. He tore a piece from the block and handed it to her.

Jake knelt then before the campfire and poured a cup of coffee from the metal pot that was sitting on a hearth stone.

"Coffee?" He held the cup out to her.

Meara took the cup and nodded a silent thank you. She took a bite from the cheese, took a sip of coffee. She looked about; at her companions, at the row of shacks, at the dark shadows that were beyond the reach of the firelight.

This was it. In a few minutes they would follow a side-passage to some distant landing, a thread to another world, and Jake would cut that thread free. They would in all likelihood be trapped forever in the other world. She would never see home again. She would never see her mother again.

If she really believed that, Meara was certain that she would be much more afraid than she felt. She was anxious, but not overly so. That was because somewhere deep in her heart she believed they would find a way home, a way back to Serpent's Keep.

After all, Jake had done it before. When everyone said that Jake was gone forever, she had known that he would return. And he had.

Why should this time be any different?

She ate the last of her cheese. Jake handed her a piece of bread.

"Are you ready?" he asked her.

"I am." Meara ate from the bread. "I just have to get my pack."

Tobias stood with his own backpack in hand. He slipped it on. "Let's not dawdle, then."

"Yes sir." Meara ate the last of her bread, washed it down with the last of her coffee. She went back into the shack to get her gear while Jake put out the campfire.

Ready then, they left the human quarter and started across the village's central plaza to the Roundhouse housing the passage stones. Two dragons stood watch outside the wide opening, even at this early hour. They said nothing, made no move, as Tobias, Jake and Meara went inside.

Tobias and Meara moved off to one side, let Jake approach the circle of six daises that were standing in the center of the room, each podium with its own passage stone. Each was the key to a unique thread in the hub that underlay the Village of the Dragons. He walked the circle, looking at the geometric symbols engraved on each stone. He stopped at the third that he came to.

"This one," he said. On the stone was the symbol the Ancient Guardian had directed him to look for.

Tobias and Meara circled the room and came up beside him. Meara took hold of Jake's arm, Tobias rested a hand on his shoulder. Jake looked from one to the other, let out a nervous breath.

"Luck to us, then," he said. If the thread was still there, the side-passage should take them to the landing and the world where they would likely spend the rest of their lives, if he was successful.

He had been in this position once before.

"Let us be off, nephew," said Tobias.

Jake looked at Meara. "Last chance, Meara."

In answer, Meara took hold of Jake's wrist and lifted his hand to the stone. She had made her choice long ago, back when she first insisted that he needed her as a guide into the Outland, back at the start of his first quest.

The journey through this passage was no different than any other. They were quickly enveloped in white, awash in a rush of light. Moments later they stepped out into a large clearing, the ground covered in a dry, mulchy layer of dead leaves and dry twigs. Beyond the clearing was a thinly treed forest of alder and scattered patches of fern and salal. The canopy was open enough to allow the sun's rays to reach the forest floor.

"Are we home?" asked Meara. "This looks like—"

"The Outland?" asked Jake. "I don't think so."

"Not the Outland that you know, my dear," said Tobias.

Jake pointed to the only trailhead leading away from the clearing. "This way."

"What are we looking for?" asked Meara.

"Haven't a clue."

Chapter Fifteen

The trail emptied at the foot of the steps leading up to the front door of a temple. It had been an easy two hour walk through a thinly treed forest that looked very much like the Outland back home.

"This looks promising," said Jake, admiring the temple.

"And familiar," said Meara. This temple had none of the additions that had been incorporated into the temple near Serpent's Keep, but the main structure looked much the same. "On the outside, anyway."

Tobias appeared distracted. "I expect we'll find much the same within as well," he said.

Jake led the way up the steps and to the door. He knocked. After half a minute with no response, he pushed down on the handle and pushed the door open.

The foyer was identical to that of the other temple, likely as all the temples. He called out, and when there was no answer, he tried again. Again there was no response.

"No one home," he said to the others. "Abandoned?"

It may or may not have been abandoned, but the foyer at least was clean and neat, with nothing to indicate the temple was being neglected.

Jake looked from one hallway to another, chose one and started into it. Tobias held out a welcoming hand to Meara for her to follow Jake, and he brought up the rear.

The way grew darker as they worked their way deeper into the temple, with the only light coming from narrow windows in the empty rooms they passed. They worked their way to the temple library. As the rest of the temple, this library was very similar to the one they all were familiar with. There were several tables in the center of the room, and the walls were lined floor to ceiling with shelves weighed heavy with old and very old books. Midway along the left wall was the honeycomb of diamond-shaped cubby holes filled with scroll tubes. A set of tall, narrow windows were evenly spaced along the far wall.

Jake looked about the room, then walked over and stood near one of the tables. He looked disappointed.

"What were you hoping to find, Jake?" asked Tobias.

"I'm not sure," said Jake. "I figured if there was a clue, it would be here."

"A logical assumption." Tobias worked his way to another table. He pulled out a chair and sat down.

"What now, sirs?" asked Meara.

Jake shook his head and sat on the corner of the table. He studied the room. "I still think it's here."

Meara began to wander about. "Eerie. Really eerie. It looks so much like ours."

"That it does," said Jake.

"Could that be the clue you're looking for, sir? The library, the temple, just like ours?"

"It's no coincidence that one of the temples is here." Jake looked over at Tobias. "Here, where the Ancient Guardian sent us."

"Coincidence, no. I wouldn't think so," said Tobias.

"You said there were a number of temples."

"That I did," said Tobias. "Six, actually; all very similar in design. As you see."

"And the Ancient Guardian was behind their creation..."

"That he was." Tobias leaned back and casually folded his arms across his chest. "Once the gates had been realized, and to some extent the secondary threads, Aldwyn sought to establish a society that existed external to humans and Jahai, a brotherhood that would stand outside and bear witness."

Meara gave a smile from across the room. "Master Peter has said as much."

"Yes, well... that was the original purpose of the brotherhood, and of their temples."

"It changed? The purpose?" asked Jake.

"The origin was lost over the centuries. And so the purpose has taken on less meaning."

Jake absently watched as Meara continued to wander the library, looking at the books on the shelves, stopping and looking at the tubes of scrolls resting in the diamond-shaped honeycomb shelves.

He moved to the chair and sat down, looked across the table to Tobias. "Okay... so how does this tie to what we need to do?" he asked.

"It doesn't. At least not directly."

"And indirectly?"

"Well, Aldwyn sent you here to isolate Janice from the rest of the web."

"Yes," Jake urged.

"To this temple; to isolate this temple from the rest of the web."

"Okay..."

"Therefore, both this temple and Janice are in this little corner of the web."

Jake frowned. "That's indirect, all right."

Tobias straightened in his chair, rested his elbows on the table. "And yet..."

"Yes?"

"I do not believe it is as simple as Aldwyn has made it out to be," said Tobias. "The key to isolating this part of the web lay not in the connecting thread itself, but in the temples."

"I don't understand," said Jake. "What do you mean, the temples?"

"The six temples were originally all in one location, in one Outland. Once completed, Aldwyn sent them out across the web as part of the original purpose, so that the brotherhood could *'bear witness'*, as he described it."

Meara stepped back to the table. "I get it," she said. "Serpent's Keep, the Outland, the Temple."

"Sent there by Aldwyn centuries ago," said Tobias, wearing a half-smile.

That explains a lot about Serpent's Keep, thought Jake.

"Are you saying that I need to bring the six temples back together?"

"Perhaps so," said Tobias. "Aldwyn sent them out along special threads. Those threads, having no other purpose, no doubt remain; the temples remain connected. They all have a connection to each other, and to this place. There were stories, even back then, that the Outland was alone in the universe, isolated in the web; hence its name."

The Outland...

Tobias continued. "Perhaps if the Outland was brought together again, the temples were returned home, that may sever the thread that brought us here today."

Jake rested his elbows on the table and rubbed his face with the palms of his hands.

"Okay, let's say that's so. Why didn't Aldwyn just tell me that?"

"He didn't tell you how to disconnect the thread, did he?"

"He told me the way would show itself."

Tobias unfolded his arms, straightened and sat forward in his chair. "And I believe it has," he stated calmly.

"Again, why not just tell me?"

"Asking you to disconnect the thread and trap yourself here is one thing, Jake," said Tobias. "But the six temples and their corresponding Outlands are populated."

Jake realized what that meant. "Oh," he said.

"Oh, my," said Meara. "It's not just us. We'll be trapping everyone here."

"I believe so," said Tobias.

"Serpent's Keep?" she asked.

"Serpent's Keep is an integral part of the Outland."

Jake let his arms slide from the table. There was a lot to take in here; six temples, one unified Outland. By bringing them together, this isolated corner of the web would be cut off from the rest of the universe, and the thread they had traveled through to get here would separate from the rest of the web.

Jake looked up from the table. "Janice isn't here," he stated. "Not yet."

"I believe she has made one of the other temples her home base," said Tobias.

By bringing the temples together home to a unified Outland, I will bring Janice here as well.

When Jake came into the mess hall, Meara was already sitting at one of the tables eating from their rations.

"Good morning, Meara." He sat at the table opposite her, sorted through the rations and picked out a cloth-wrapped block of cheese. He unwrapped it and tore a piece from the block and tossed it in his mouth. "We're still on rations, I see."

Meara took a drink from her glass of water. "I could find no food."

"I didn't really think you would." This temple may have been left in good condition, but its occupants had abandoned it long ago. "Have you seen Tobias?"

"He told me he was going to meditate."

Jake nodded absently. He selected a bag of dried fruit, opened it and began picking through the bits of fruit.

Once they did what needed doing, they were going to have to go in search of a food source. Their rations were running low.

Jake chose not to bring that up just now.

Meara indicated the dried fruit, meats and cheese blocks that were set out on the table. There wasn't much there.

"This is all there is, sir."

Okay, so let's bring it up...

Jake picked out another piece of fruit. If this Outland was anything like their Outland, there was food out there. Meara had been good at finding what they needed during their earlier quest.

Jake looked carefully at a dried apricot and took a bite from it. "It'll do," he said.

"Sir?" Meara asked.

Jake poured a glass of water from one of the canteens, then refilled her glass as well. "What about water?" he asked.

"Pump in the kitchen," she said. "It works."

"Good, good..." Jake drank deep from his glass. They ate quietly from their rations. "Meditating, huh?"

"Yes sir," said Meara. "He does that."

"Yes. I know."

Tobias had been committed to meditating in the mornings while he and Jake were traveling the side-passages, but since coming out of the threads hadn't meditated once that Jake knew of.

Meara closed the ration packet she had been eating from. "I think I'll take a walk outside, sir; I'd like to get a look at the grounds."

"Good idea," said Jake. "We'll meet back here later."

Jake watched her leave the mess hall, then finished up his breakfast of cheese and dried fruit. Leaving Tobias to his meditation and Meara to her walk then, Jake returned to the library.

He didn't really have a plan in mind; rather he didn't have anywhere else to look. If there was a thread to be pulled anywhere in the temple, wouldn't it be in the repository of all knowledge?

He felt himself drawn there.

Entering the dimly lit room, the morning's gray light was barely pushing through the tall, narrow windows on the opposite wall. He started along the near wall of shelves. He stopped after several steps and looked over at the tables in the center of the room.

There was a large, loosely-rolled scroll sitting on one of the tables, bound with thin twine. He was certain that it hadn't been there before. Jake had been the last to leave the library the night before, and he doubted that either Tobias or Meara had returned during the night. And in any case, would either of them have left a scroll on the table, loosely bound in twine?

Jake looked uneasily about the library. There didn't appear to be anyone hiding in the shadows. Could there be someone else, somewhere else in the temple? Absolutely. The temple was a big place, with a lot of empty rooms.

Jake grew more uneasy still. He moved apprehensively over to the table. He looked quickly about the room again, then back to the scroll. The parchment was deeply yellowed. It was old, very old.

A pull of one end of the twine and he was able to unroll the scroll and smooth it out flat across the table.

It was a map. There was a temple displayed there. Another there... and another there. Six temples, set across what must be the unified Outland.

Jake looked up from the scroll, looked warily about the library, then back over his shoulder toward the door leading out into the hall.

He was alone.

He looked down again at the ancient map.

This was it. The key. Somehow, this was it. Whatever *it* was. And someone had left it here for him to find.

Martin and Janice stood before the table, looking down at an ancient scroll. There were several bright lamps in the room, pushing shadows away. The shelves of the library were empty, all the books and scrolls having long since been removed.

Janice didn't much like this old temple, but it did serve well enough as a base of operations.

"It was just sitting here," said Martin. "No one knows where it came from, how it got here. It was just... here."

Janice looked up from the map, glanced around the room at the empty shelves. Further down one wall, the honeycomb of scroll cubbyholes was as empty as the rest of the room.

She looked back at the map. Six temples were displayed in an expansive forest landscape.

She knew what this was meant to represent. They all knew the stories.

Aldwyn's temples.

Janice looked up again, looked about the room again. A hot tingling numbness coursed through her body.

How did this get here?

Aldwyn stood before the portal hovering in the very center of the round chamber. The portal shimmered, the earlier image slowly washing away, a new image forming.

An image now of a temple ruin, piles of stone rubble and half-rotted wooden beams. A dragon sat high on the broken remains of a wall. Its eyes were closed, its wings were folded along its sides.

Aldwyn lifted a hand before him, slowly rolled his fingers. A large scroll materialized in his hand, yellow parchment loosely bound with thin twine.

This would be scroll number six...

He held the scroll out, midway between himself and the portal. It vanished, leaving Aldwyn's hand empty now before him.

§

The winged dragon felt a tingling in his mind.

Lamal opened his eyes. He tilted his head, looked down from his perch atop the broken wall down to the rubble below amongst the temple ruin. There was something there. There was something there that hadn't been there before.

Lamal stretched out one wing, then the other. Holding both out then for balance, he lifted himself off the wall and dropped down to the rubble. He landed a few yards from the object.

It was a scroll. He had heard of such things. He had seen one once before, though he couldn't remember when or where.

He took a step forward. He reached a claw out to the thing that shouldn't be there.

Janice reached out and brushed a hand across the parchment that was spread out before her.

Jake leaned forward, laid a hand palm down on the ancient scroll.

Tobias was sitting on a wooden chair in the monk cell, his eyes closed, his hands resting in his lap. There was a narrow cot on his left, a small window set high on the wall behind him. The cell door in front of him stood open.

The universe was quiet. Tobias was one with it and yet outside of it, alone and yet a part of everything.

Something had brushed at his mind…

He turned his head slightly.

Something was there… something reached out to him from the quiet.

Tobias opened his eyes.

Mr. Griffin moved to the edge of the second floor deck. The streets of the village were quiet. Few could see what he saw, isolated as they were by the high stone walls that enclosed Serpent's Keep. Most would live their lives without ever seeing the lands of the Outland beyond those walls.

He heard the door behind him open and close. Mrs. Hodges came up beside him. They both stood silent for a few moments.

"Just as you said, Mrs. Hodges," he said evenly.

From the mansion's upper floor deck it was possible to see the Outland beyond the village walls; a mix of fir and oak and alder, the canopy hid the numerous dangers of the strange land. To the west, the spires of the temple rose above the treetops in the distance.

There was something different this day. The canopy had always had a familiar pattern of evergreen and deciduous, of color and texture and shadow. That pattern was different now, the change evident to anyone who spent time on this deck taking in this unique view and the warmth of the afternoon sun.

And there was something more...

The spires of the temple, poking up through this newly unfamiliar canopy, were nearer to the village.

The temple... it was closer. How was that possible?

Looking to the north, Mrs. Hodges indicated something in the distance. "Look," she said.

It was another pair of spires, just visible rising above the canopy.

It was another temple.

"The Outland has been reshaped," said Brother John.

"That and more," said Master Peter.

They were standing on the roof of the east wing of the temple. From here they could see a great distance in every direction.

More than simply reshaped...

The Outland, always vast, stretched out now to the horizon, to all horizons, the treetop canopy a blanket that lay over the landscape as far as the eye could see.

Serpent's Keep was there, visible only as a break in the trees to the east, as always... but there was something wrong about it. Studying it now, the sight of it made Peter uneasy.

And then he realized that the village was considerably closer than it had been only yesterday, much closer than it should be.

Looking off to his left, he saw something else that shouldn't be there. Poking up through the canopy were the spires of yet another temple.

"Are you up for a walk, John?" he asked.

Brother John was looking at the same temple spires. They looked to be a morning's easy walk, assuming there were no difficulties traveling through the woods.

"Certainly, Master Peter."

Natan stood alone in the center of the village plaza. A heavily muscled Thrauhm dragon watched from a discrete distance, two others stood watch at the roundhouse, but the village was otherwise quiet.

Natan's attention was on the sky. It was as still and quiet as the village. Sensing movement near the roundhouse, he glanced once at the building, focused again on the sky.

Khol came out of the roundhouse and walked over to stand beside the Jahai leader. He did not look up at the sky, did not look directly at Natan. He studied the village around them.

"The thread is no more," he stated matter-of-factly.

"They were successful, then."

"We can assume so, Natan." Khol's expression was stiff, unyielding. "Natan... it was our last functioning passage stone."

Natan said nothing to that. He already knew the other passage stones had gone silent.

The silhouette of a Lynhaur dragon glided above them, slowly circled over the village before coming down half a dozen paces in front of Natan and Khol. It folded its wings against its side and strode awkwardly to stand before them.

"What news, friend?" asked Natan.

"Changed," said the dragon. "All changed."

Natan nodded gravely, his fears realized. He looked coolly at Khol, turned again to the flying dragon.

"Describe this change, my friend," he said.

"Trees. All trees. Only trees. Nothing. Nothing. Village... we... alone."

Chapter Sixteen

Brother John led the way across the forest floor, Master Peter two paces behind him and three brother monks bringing up the rear. They had left the trail when they were thirty minutes out from the temple, but the Outland here was easy travel, with a sparse forest and only scattered vegetation of giant fern and salal. The ground was covered in a layer of dried leaves. The day was warm but not hot; the sky, visible through the thin canopy, was a pale bluish gray.

Late in the morning, John stepped out onto a wide trail, smooth with a light-colored soil and hardy tufts of dry grass and aromatic weeds. Following this new trail would continue them in the direction of the nearby temple newly appeared.

Half an hour later they came into the clearing in front of the temple. It was much like theirs, and yet not. While the basic building structure of their own Serpent's Keep temple had been added onto a number of times over the years, this temple looked to have been unchanged since it was originally constructed.

To their left, the grounds were clear to the corner of the temple and beyond. To their right, there was a tall, green wall of a hedge that continued around the corner.

The group of monks stood silent for several long moments, taking it all in.

"Well, now that we're here…" Master Peter began. "I suppose we should see whether anyone is home." He started up the steps, Brother John following right beside him. The others waited below.

The doors ahead of them opened as Peter took the top step and reached the landing. Tobias Quigley stepped outside. He put on a welcoming smile.

"Peter, my friend; and Brother John. How good of you to drop by."

Brother John pulled the library door gently closed, leaving Master Peter to try to sort out recent events with Master Tobias and young Jacob. Walking the hall, he was again struck by just how similar this temple was to his own, and yet how so very different. This temple left him with the feeling that it wasn't lived in. It lacked the personal effects and touches, the things that one would expect to see in a sanctuary where the brotherhood walked the halls that he now walked, that sat at the tables in the mess, that slept in the rows of monk cells, that studied in the library, conversed with one another in conference rooms. While he had no idea what had happened to these distant brothers, he had the sense that they had been gone for a very long time.

He reached the front foyer, stood in the center of the room. It was quiet. The temple was quiet. His own temple was always quiet, but not like this. There was a hollow silence to the place.

He went to the front door and stepped outside. Meara was standing below at the foot of the steps. She looked back over her shoulder, up to John on the porch.

"Hello, John. Did they throw you out?"

John seldom read Meara very well. He just assumed that she was serious. "I have little to contribute at this time."

"Uh, huh," Meara sighed tiredly. She moved away from the steps, indicated that John should follow. John took a few moments to consider whether or not it was a good idea. He finally descended the steps and walked over to where Meara waited.

They walked to the corner of the temple and then up to the tall hedge. Meara led John along the hedge to an open iron gate. Beyond the gate, on the other side of the hedge, was an overgrown garden of flowering shrubs, raised vegetable beds and short hedges. They walked a narrow path along the outer perimeter of the enclosed garden.

"Nice, huh?" asked Meara.

"It was, once," said John. The garden at least would qualify as a personal touch by the previous occupants of the temple.

"Yeah," Meara sighed. She brushed a hand across a large bush that pushed into the path, threatened to overwhelm the path. The garden hadn't been tended to in years. "I suppose it could use some sprucing up."

"Some."

They walked in silence for a time.

"You should have done something like this in your temple," said Meara.

"We have a vegetable garden," said John.

"Yes, but not, you know... a garden."

"Our garden suits our needs just fine, Meara."

They followed the walkway roundabout and continued into the heart of the garden.

"Master Quigley says there are six temples," said Meara.

"From his deciphering of the scrolls, Master Peter has recently deduced as much," said John. "They were created for the use of the brotherhood."

"And now Jake has brought them together again."

Brother John noted the informal reference to Jacob Quigley.

"So he's *Jake* now?"

"He insisted. He said that he didn't like me referring to him as *Master Jacob*."

"And what about Master Quigley? *Tobias*?"

They reached a stone bench. Meara brushed dried leaves from the seat and sat down.

"Master Quigley will always be Master Quigley," she said.

John agreed with a knowing half smile.

"So he shall," he said.

Brother John considered the end of the bench, brushed a lone leaf aside and sat down beside Meara. He clasped his hands in his lap. He looked across the narrow walk at the vegetation gone wild after years of neglect.

Yes, young Jacob Quigley had brought the six temples together, after being apart for who knew how long. More than that... the Outland. There had always been something distinct about the Outland. It had always stood apart from the rest of the world.

Now it was home.

And it was one. The Outland was now one; unified.

"You and your father spent a lot of time in the Outland," John observed.

"We did," Meara stated. "My father had a unique relationship with the Outland."

"I would agree. I believe he enjoyed his time out there."

"Yes. He did."

"You did not?"

"I always gave it the respect it deserved."

"I see." Brother John was looking across the walk at overgrown bush. There were several birds moving about within the branches and leaves. Juncos, he believed.

But his thoughts had already moved beyond the garden; his thoughts were beyond the hedge that enclosed the garden.

The Outland is now one...

Jake, Tobias and Master Peter were hovering over the scroll that was spread across the table. Tobias indicated one of the temples represented on the parchment.

"This is where we are," he said.

Master Peter placed a finger on another; he tapped twice. That was his temple, where he had spent much of his life. He then drew the finger across the scroll to the image of a village enclosed by a wall.

Tobias nodded. Meara would be pleased. *Serpent's Keep...*

He looked across at Jake. The boy had been unusually quiet.

"Something on your mind, Jacob?"

Jake stared down at the scroll, at the landscape that it represented. What had happened?

He had placed his hand on the ancient parchment, and six temples had been pulled across an unseen web underlying the universe and brought to this place, to an Outland unified.

Is this what I had been sent here to do?

He had no doubt that this was so.

He nodded calmly at the scroll.

"You figure Janice is in one of those other temples?"

"I figure," said Tobias.

"Janice?" asked Peter.

"Kinda the reason for all this," said Jake. He folded his arms across his chest. They needed to be sure. "I suggest a tour."

"Agreed," said Tobias.

Corwin turned left out of the wider hall and moved into the narrower hallway. He followed it into the castle's inner foyer, crossed the room and opened the heavy double doors. He entered the round chamber room. The observation portal in the center of the room had gone dark, hung now there as a dull gray silhouette.

Aldwyn was standing near the French doors, looking outward, his back to the room. Corwin moved quietly across the room and stopped one step behind Aldwyn. He waited for some sign from the master of the castle. None came.

"Aldwyn?" he urged at last.

"Yes, Corwin?"

"Sir... the outside."

"Yes." Aldwyn stated calmly.

"There is nothing there. It's gone."

"Yes, Corwin. I know."

"Sir? The Dark Path? You knew, sir?"

Aldwyn turned his head and looked back at Corwin for the first time. He gave his companion a confident smile.

"All will be well, my friend."

"Of course, sir." Corwin didn't look all that reassured, despite his belief in Aldwyn. "The Dark Path, sir."

A gentle smile from Aldwyn; perhaps he should have offered Corwin the chance to leave. That was no longer an option. The Dark Path was gone, and there was no other path from the castle.

He placed a hand on Corwin's arm.

"There was no other way, my friend. The greater charge necessitated a number of alterations to the web; that would include the loss of the path."

"I understand, sir," said Corwin. "We are on our own then, sir?"

"For the foreseeable future."

Corwin steeled himself. Very well. So be it.

"Dinner, sir?"

Aldwyn's smile broadened. "That would be fine, my friend."

Chapter Seventeen

Mrs. Hodges walked Serpent's Keep's main thoroughfare toward the marketplace, pulling her empty wire cart behind her. She was as yet unsure of what was happening beyond the walls of the village, but between the strange skies and shifting Outland landscape, the world was obviously changing and she wanted to make sure that the Quigley Estate was prepared. The supply room and pantry were both well-stocked, but they could do with more perishables.

It was early afternoon and the thoroughfare was crowded with villagers. From the bits of conversation that she heard in passing, a few were concerned with what had happened beyond the walls, but most had no idea that anything had changed. Most were simply glad that the atmospheric disturbances had died down and they were taking the opportunity to enjoy the pleasant weather of the past few days.

Turning into the marketplace, she was surprised to see that many of the booths were already closed for the day and there were only a few shoppers milling about.

She noticed then Meara and a robed monk standing near the closed booth of Meara's mother.

When had they returned?

Mrs. Hodges dragged her cart across the plaza. As she drew nearer she recognized the monk that was standing with Meara. It was Brother John.

There was no sign of Master Quigley or young Jacob.

"Meara! You're back."

"Yes, ma'am," said Meara. "Just this hour."

"And you are well, I see. And what of the others? What of Master Quigley and Jacob?"

"Out there still, Mrs. Hodges. But not far. In the Outland."

"Ah, yes. The Outland."

"More than a few changes there, Mrs. Hodges." Meara indicated the closed booth. "I see my mother closed early today."

Mrs. Hodges acknowledged that with a nod, then looked to the monk, who had stood silent until now. She hadn't seen John since he had left the village to join the brotherhood.

"John. It is good to see you."

"Thank you, Mrs. Hodges," said John. "You appear well, as always."

"Tough as leather and just as long-lived," she said. "And what of Master Peter? He and I chanced to have a conversation not so long ago."

"He is with Master Tobias and his young nephew; they are on a bit of an explore."

And with that the discussion turned to the six temples and the reintegration of the Outland.

"Rather mystifying," sighed Brother John.

"Mystifying, perhaps," said Mrs. Hodges. "But to be honest, it does explain a lot."

"That it does," said Meara. "If only my father was here to witness it."

"I believe that Master Gyles knew more than he knew," said Mrs. Hodges. She looked again to John. "Speaking of family, John... have you seen yours?"

"Not yet, ma'am." John looked uncomfortable.

"Do so." Mrs. Hodges gave him a stern look. "I shall be asking them about you later."

"Of course, Mrs. Hodges. I shall."

"Good."

Janice was sitting on the top step of the temple's front porch, her elbows on her knees, her hands clasped, fingers intertwined. She was both physically and mentally drained, having come down now from running nonstop for so long. She would never admit it, not to anyone, but there was a part of her that was relieved it was over. She could stop now. She could rest.

And it was over. She was sure of that. She knew what had happened and what it meant. Aldwyn, safely ensconced in his high castle, had sent his surrogates out to restore his beloved Outland and once again isolate her, imprison her here and prevent her from completing her mission.

Martin came into the clearing from an overgrown trailhead directly opposite the temple steps. He had been out there for more than an hour, wandering the landscape of the Outland. Janice felt sorry for him, and couldn't help but give him a sympathetic smile as he walked up to the bottom step.

Martin had desperately wanted for there to be no difference out there, had wanted to return with news that all was well, that all was as it had been, that the way was yet open to travel the web.

"I am sorry, Janice," he said.

"Poor Martin," said Janice. "We already knew as much."

"But couldn't there be a way... couldn't there be a portal, some path... some way?"

Janice took a long, deep breath, slowly shook her head. "Not this time."

It took Martin another half minute to finally accept what she had said, even already knowing the truth. He climbed the bottom step then, turned about and sat on the steps below Janice. The two sat quietly, each in their own thoughts, until the sound of twigs snapping pushed in on the silence.

They looked up in time to see Tobias and Jake come into the clearing.

"I've been expecting you," said Janice.

"Hello, Janice." Tobias looked at the temple, back to Janice sitting on the step. "You all settled in?"

"I don't see as there's much of a rush," she said. "Do you?"

"I do not."

A shadow passed across the clearing. Tobias lifted his gaze from Janice to the sky overhead. The dark silhouette of a flying dragon glided above them.

"Isn't that the dragon we saw on the Dark Path?" Jake asked quietly.

"Jamal," said Tobias. "To be expected. He returned with his temple."

Evening had come. Lamal drifted casually in the graying sky. The expanded landscape of the Outland passed beneath him, growing darker and more shadowed as day turned to dusk.

Up ahead then, he could see a darker gash that lay across the landscape.

Lamal reached the Great Ravine, circled and looked down into the gorge. Fellow dragons were coming out of their cliff dwellings to welcome the evening; silhouettes gliding above the forest canopy that blanketed the ravine floor.

Lamal circled downward as he slowly descended into the ravine.

Chapter Eighteen

Master Peter closed the leather-bound book and slid his chair back from the table. He looked about the library, stood then and carried the large volume back to the shelves set into the back wall.

The library; his library; his temple. Home.

He had visited three of the other temples over the last few days, having returned home just the evening before. It was good to be home. As similar as the temples may appear on the surface, they were actually very different. It wasn't just the superficial changes that had been made over the centuries. There was something much deeper, something integrated within the very fabric of each temple. The brotherhood of each had made each temple their own in very personal and subjective ways, and this individual quality was felt the moment one stepped through the front doors.

Walking the halls now, that which made this temple home for Peter felt warm and real. He was one with the temple, as were his brethren. Such was the heart and substance of the brotherhood.

He poked his head into the mess, saw that lunch wasn't quite ready. Brother Steven held up a hand, indicating five more minutes.

Peter continued down the hall, turned down the narrow passage to the north tower. He climbed the circular staircase up to the top landing, then the ladder up to the roof access. Once on the roof, he walked across to the roof edge and took in the scene that was spread out before him.

The view was the same view that he had been witnessing from this rooftop for decades, and yet it was now very different. The sky overhead was a cloudless blue, hovering above a canopy of evergreen and oak and alder. The village of Serpent's Keep was there, visible as an open expanse of the Outland to the east.

But the Outland was different. The Outland had always reached to the horizon, but the horizon appeared much further now. And then there was the very configuration of the canopy. The pattern of evergreen and deciduous had changed.

And of course the distance between the temple and Serpent's Keep had changed. It was more than just illusion; those who had walked the trail reported that the village was indeed much nearer.

And then there were the spires poking up through the canopy, visible evidence of the presence of the arrival of the other temples. From here Peter could see the spires of two of those temples, both of them to the north. He had visited both, and one other that wasn't visible from here. Janice had been found in one; another was empty, the third was home to fellow monks, distant members of the brotherhood. Of the two temples that he had not visited, he had been informed that one was a ruin, the last occupied by another group of monks.

Brother John came out onto the roof and stepped up beside Peter.

"Hello, John. How was your visit?"

"Fine, Master Peter. Mrs. Hodges sends her best."

"A lovely woman."

"Yes." John had returned from the village the day before, but this was his first chance to meet with Peter. And it hadn't been chance. He had sought him out.

"Master Peter, when you have a moment, can you drop by the meeting chamber?"

"I'm sure the arrangements are fine, brother," said Peter.

"Nonetheless." John waited.

"Very well," Peter sighed. Movement in the nearby trees below caught his attention. Looking closely, he saw a line of figures traveling along the trail toward them. "And here they come," he said.

Looking below, Brother John watched as a group of monks from one of the nearby temples came into the clearing. "They're early," he said.

"Invite them to lunch," said Peter. "A shared meal is a wonderful opportunity to begin forming a bond between our two temples ahead of the meeting."

"Yes, sir." John was nervous. This was to be the first of what would no doubt be a number of meetings between the two temples and it was important that it go well. He wished that he had been given more warning, more time to prepare. "I shall see to it," he said, started back across the rooftop to the access door.

"John," Peter called after him.

"Sir?" John stopped and turned back.

"Your visit to the village. I understand you had a chance to visit your family."

"Yes sir," John said, a bit hesitantly.

"It went well?" Peter asked. "Not to pry, not looking for details."

"It went well enough, Master." John's family hadn't been very supportive with John's decision to join the brotherhood, and he hadn't seen them since he left the village for the brief journey to the temple.

"Good enough, Brother John. I hope I haven't made you uncomfortable."

"Not at all, sir. Thank you, sir."

Peter gave a dismissive nod. "I'll be down presently."

"Thank you, sir." John turned about and left the rooftop.

Master Peter focused his attention again to the Outland beyond the temple grounds.

He was looking forward to this new world.

Tobias Quigley descended the stairs from the second floor. He crossed the front hall to the archway and entered the kitchen in the back of Quigley Mansion.

It was good to be home.

As much as he enjoyed his ventures out there... anywhere out there, coming home always felt good; this time all the more so. His trips were usually weeks in length. Not so this time; beginning with the quest, then his time spent trapped in a landing, then the side-passage travels with Jake, finally the journey on the Dark Path and beyond, had lasted several years.

Yes, it was good to be home. He planned on staying a while.

Mr. Griffin and Meara turned to him when Tobias came into the kitchen. They looked to have been in conversation.

"Mr. Griffin, Miss Gyles." Tobias walked around the island counter and took a glass down from the cupboard. "How goes your morning?"

"Just fine, Master Quigley," Mr. Griffin answered. "Can I help you with anything?"

"Nope." Tobias found a pitcher of iced tea in the refrigerator, filled his glass. He sat at the counter. "Just getting reacquainted with the place."

"Of course, sir."

Tobias took a drink from his glass, looked across at Meara. "How about you, my dear? Good to be home?"

"Yes sir."

There wasn't much fervor behind the answer.

"Uh, huh." Tobias held back a grin. "You can't wait to get back out there, eh?"

"I can do without the daily risks to life and limb, sir."

Tobias slowly nodded, took another drink from his iced tea. He sat the glass down on the counter in front of him. "You've earned a bit of peace, Meara. Enjoy it."

"I shall, Master Quigley." Meara looked to Mr. Griffin, back to Tobias. "I should return to my duties."

Tobias lifted his glass. "Of course. Good morning to you."

Meara nodded to Tobias and left the kitchen.

"Her last day?" Tobias asked Mr. Griffin.

"Tomorrow, I believe."

"I wish her well."

"Of course, sir."

The back door opened and Mrs. Hodges entered the kitchen, pulling her wire cart behind her.

"Ah, Master Quigley," she said. She swung the cart around and parked it. "Lunch in half an hour."

"I can hardly wait, Mrs. Hodges."

"You've little choice in the matter. Half an hour."

"Yes, ma'am. I'll do my best." Tobias gave a side glance and wink to Mr. Griffin, turned again to Mrs. Hodges. "Yep. Good to be home."

I think I'll stay a while.

Jake leaned back in his chair and let Sparta refill his coffee cup. Looking about the café, He gave a nod to Mr. Dante, who was sitting at his regular table. There was a young couple sitting at a table near one of the windows, deep in conversation.

"Wallace will have your soup and sandwich ready in a couple of minutes," said Sparta.

"I'm not in any hurry." Jake took a sip from his coffee.

"Does that mean you're home for a while?"

Jake didn't really want to discuss his plans with Sparta.

"Let's just say I have time for a long lunch," he said.

"I see." She rested one hand on her hip and gave him a playful look. "Do you have something against settling down, Jake?"

"Not at all, Sparta," he said. "It's just that events always seem to get in the way."

"Events do look to have your name on 'em, that's for true." Sparta saw Wallace put Jake's lunch up. She gave Jake a side-glance as she went to fetch it. "Soup and sandwich, coming up."

Sheriff Smith came into the café half a minute later as Sparta returned with Jake's bowl and plate.

"Hello, Sheriff," Jake prompted. "Pull up a chair."

"Thank you, Mister Quigley." The sheriff looked to Sparta as he sat down. "Just coffee, Sparta."

Jake swallowed a spoonful of soup and took a bite of his sandwich, looked across the table.

"All quiet in the village?" he asked, though he knew the answer. There really wasn't much change before and after recent happenings, particularly once the skies settled down.

The village was the village.

"Back to normal, for the most part," said the sheriff.

"That's good."

"So what are your plans now, Jake?"

"I thought I'd try my hand at surveying. The Outland needs mapping."

"Ah, so you're off again."

"A few short trips, to start; then, we'll see. We'll go from there." Jake watched Sparta bring a cup for the sheriff. She filled it from the carafe and quietly left. "But then, I'm guessing you already knew that."

"I may have heard something about it." He turned his cup about and picked it up by the handle. He took a sip. "Nothing covert. Meara's mother told me."

"I hope she's not upset." Jake knew that the woman had lost her husband to the Outland.

"Not at all. She knows her daughter."

"Good to hear," said Jake. "Meara was great out there."

"No doubts there. It's easy to see her father in her."

Jake took a bite of his sandwich. "I get that," he said.

"And she's a good choice to team up with on your surveying," said the sheriff.

"Yeah," said Jake. "I didn't really have much say in the matter."

Sheriff Smith grinned as he finished the last of his coffee. He turned down a refill from Sparta and slid his chair back.

"I should get back at it." He stood, pushed his chair under the table. "So, you're heading out day after tomorrow?"

Meara's mother had been quite the informant.

"That's the plan," said Jake.

"Maybe I'll see you before you leave." The sheriff gave a nod good-bye, stepped away from the table and left the café.

"Pie?" Sparta was standing beside Jake, watching as he put the last of his sandwich in his mouth.

"Excuse me?" Jake mumbled through his food.

"Pie. Apple."

"Um... okay."

"Coming right up." Sparta started away.

Jake leaned back, glanced about the café. Mr. Dante was eating pie. The two sitting at the window were eating pie. A woman at the small table in the corner, *when had she come in?* was eating pie.

Life in Serpent's Keep wasn't going to be bad at all.

Jahai Encyclopedia

The Jahai are the twelve dragon species of the four habitable planets of the Jahai system.

The Jahai had joined with Tobias Quigley and stood watch for a thousand years as Guardians of the Artifacts, the components of the gate that had been distributed to the Other Worlds by Tobias.

The Jahai Species

Bentai
The Bentai are much more humanoid in physical appearance than other Jahai species. They tend to be a head taller than the average human, with sloping shoulders, a large head and protruding snout. They have extraordinarily long fingers ending in curved claws. Unlike other Jahai species, Bentai wear clothing, albeit simple, usually open leather vests and calf-length skirts. The Bentai are the primary administrative class of the Jahai. The leader of the Jahai is Bentai.

Lynhaur
One of several of the flying species of dragon. Colored in multiple shades of green and brown, the Lynhaur are sleek, but with powerful hind legs, slightly smaller front legs that can be used as arms and hands. Their leathery wings are folded and bundled on their back when not in use.

Thrauhm
Thrauhm are heavy, well-muscled, with thick legs and neck, are broad chested and have an overlarge head. They are intelligent but have limited language and simple speech.

Zelhaur
The Zelhaur are a lizard-like species well-suited to the desert, their home environment the arid southern continent of the innermost world of the Jahai planetary system. The Zelhaur body is slung between short, powerful legs, its belly and tail held up off the sand.

Slyruhm
The amphibian species of the Jahai dragon; sleek, silky water serpent at home in the water. The Slyruhm has a small head in relation to its long, undulating serpentine neck, a sharp protruding chin and large dark eyes. They are articulate, well-spoken.

Jehnlaur
Gentle and slight, the Jehnlaur are thin and agile, bipedal with delicate hands and fingers. They mother their young for several years. They frequently care for and are protective of the Chenling species.

Venerahn
Long, very slender body, spindly legs; overlarge wings are nearly transparent. They are highly cerebral, live most of their lives alone.

Chenling
Sometimes referred to as "Little Ones" by humans, Chenling have all the dragon features of the larger Jahai species, but are no larger than midsize dogs. They commonly live in groups in underground tunnels and labyrinths, but will also individually attach to other dragons or humans.

The Four Friends
The four distinct species of the fourth planet in the Jahai system are referred to as "The Four Friends". They seldom leave their home world, are seldom seen by other Jahai species, and very little is known about them.